THE ARMY DOC'S BABY SECRET

CHARLOTTE HAWKES

MILLS & BOON

First published in Great Britain 2019
by Mills & Boon, an imprint of HarperCollins*Publishers*
1 London Bridge Street, London, SE1 9GF

Large Print edition 2020

© 2019 Charlotte Hawkes

ISBN: 978-0-263-08537-2

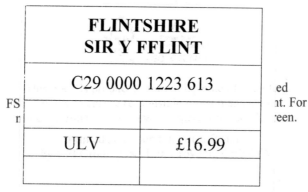

To my husband. I may forget
birthday cards (in my defence,
I remembered one last year—
I just forgot to sign it),
but I can dedicate a book to you.

XXX

CHAPTER ONE

DR ANTONIA FARRINGDALE was adroit at smelling trouble.

She had first learned it at her father's knee, watching the oft-churning grey expanse of the Atlantic Ocean from the salt-sprayed windows of Westlake lifeboat station, as her mother piloted a boat out for a rescue. Learning to read the signs for when the crew was in for an easy night, or the omens for when they could expect an arduous night of dangerous shouts.

She had honed it as a doctor, often knowing instinctively with her patients when she was hearing horses, and those rare occasions when she was hearing zebras.

And she had perfected it as a battlefield trauma doctor working from twelve-by-twelve tents of field hospitals on missions in whichever conflict-hardened country *du jour* she was in.

Yes, she could certainly smell trouble.

So why, she wondered as she peered uneasily into the hallway at Delburn Bay lifeboat station—a mere hour and a half further up the coast from Westlake, and therefore the closest she'd managed to get herself to *going home* in over a decade—did she smell it so unnervingly strongly, right at this instant?

Immobile yet alert, she stood in her doorway. Scarcely even daring to breathe as her eyes scanned for anything out of the ordinary.

But the sea was agreeably calm beyond the launch slipway, and the corridors were quiet, most of the crew being volunteers who had day jobs but who would be at the station within minutes if they were called to be. There was nothing there which should set her chest thumping the way that it was.

Unless a guilty conscience counted.

Shaking her head as if that would be sufficient to dislodge the censorious thought, Antonia ducked back into the medical supply room, which doubled as her consultation room and office whenever she was on site as the station's new Medical Officer, telling herself it was more likely to be just her overactive imagination.

Telling herself that she had nothing to feel guilty about.

Telling herself...what? That she'd made the right choices—as impossible as they had been—five years ago?

It was true, but it didn't help. It never really had. She still felt like a terrible person.

But then, wasn't that why she was back here? To set the record straight.

Spinning around on the ball of her foot, Antonia strode determinedly back into her office and consultation room even as her mind skittered down the coast to Westlake, back to the past, to the man who had finally brought her back home now. Or, at least, that mere ninety minutes up the coast from home. A man to whom she owed the two biggest apologies of her entire life. Neither of which she had any idea how to even *begin* to make.

Which was why she'd taken a job at Delburn Bay's lifeboat station, rather than back at Westlake. The distance provided her with a much-needed buffer to allow her to pick the words she was going to use when she finally plucked up the courage to drive down the coast and face…*him.*

Ezekiel Jackson.

As though she hadn't already had five years to work out what to say. The drumming in her head intensified, causing her to pinch the bridge of her nose. Not that it helped.

'You're supposed to be working,' Antonia muttered irritably into the silent room. 'Not looking for ghosts.'

Her heeled boots clacked harshly as she strode back to her desk, and she pulled her lips into a grim line as she selected the next file from her pile. Technically she didn't start officially for another month, but it was a voluntary position and they were desperate for someone to settle in. And it was better than being in her father's small house, avoiding his concerned glances and all his unspoken questions, which nonetheless echoed loudly.

Gratefully she slid down into the uncomfortable swivel chair and began to read the notes. Work had always been her salvation. Unsurprising, then, that she was absorbed within minutes.

'So it's true.'

The rich, smouldering, all too familiar voice seemed to charge the room, as Antonia jerked her head up so fast that a *crack* and a stinging sensation ripped through her neck.

She wasn't prepared. She wasn't *ready*.

If a deep chasm had opened up beneath her feet and sent her hurtling down to the earth's dense, super-hot core, it couldn't have made her any more frantic.

Zeke.

Had the air been sucked out of her lungs? Her body? The very room itself? It certainly felt like it. She couldn't breathe, let alone speak, and it was all she could do to keep her mouth clamped shut rather than open and close it like a fish caught out in one of the rock pools out on the sands.

How she managed to stand—to face him—she would never know. Yet suddenly she was on her feet, her fingers braced against the cold, flat wood of her desk to stop the dizziness from winning out. She certainly had no idea how she managed to respond to him.

'True?'

Thank goodness for the open window, which let her suck in deep lungsful of sea air—its salty, tangy taste dancing obliviously on her tongue—as she tried to quell the wave of nausea that crested in her chest.

Damn it if Zeke didn't look every last bit as commanding, and dangerous, and *male*, as she remembered. His hair was longer now. At least, longer than the close-to-the-scalp cut he'd sported as a Special Forces soldier back then. Enough that she might actually be able to feel it between her fingers.

If she wanted to. Which she didn't. Of course she didn't...*because that would be pathetic*.

Desperately, urgently, Antonia reminded herself of that last night, five years ago. He'd been telling her for months that he didn't love her, that he'd never loved her, but that had been the night when she'd finally believed him. Because it hadn't been the words that had convinced her, rather it had been that hard, disgusted look in his cold eyes as they'd bored into her without a trace of softness or love behind them.

Even now, at the mere memory, a pain shot through her heart as though it were folding in on itself.

And then she looked into Zeke's face and suddenly her heart kicked out again, straightening itself out and pounding so loudly within her chest that she was afraid it could be heard.

He was a few years older, maybe, but that face was just as sharp, and masculine, and devastating as it had always been. Those cool blue eyes could still pierce through any soul, and that strong jawline, which she had traced countless times over the years, still housed a mouth that had been her undoing more times than she cared to remember.

Without warning, desire zipped through her, horrifying and thrilling all at the same time. His beaten-up leathers moulded to every broad, muscled inch of him, reminding her of a time when—as teenagers—they had raced the length and breadth of the country on that prized motorbike of his.

Suddenly, she felt like that adoring kid again.

Had she really been so naïve as to believe that the mere passage of time would mean she would no longer be attracted to the man? Had she really told herself that she would be immune?

She'd convinced herself of it, yet now the mere idea that she wouldn't be affected by him was laughable.

Even his silence was dark. Edgy. Lasting only a beat but feeling like an eternity.

'That you're back.'

Another moment of silence. So thick and heavy that she almost imagined she could wear it as a cloak. Maybe one that could chase out the sudden chill that had pervaded her very bones.

Almost against her own volition, Tia let her eyes track lower. Her heart kicked up yet another gear as she fought to control the shallow breaths that jostled inside. Zeke had once been the epitome of a deadly, dangerous, ruinous barracuda.

Something she didn't care to identify pooled low in her belly at the memory of the SBS man with a body that had always defied belief and was worthy of any Rodin or Polycleitus sculpture.

If she didn't know better, she might have thought that nothing had changed. He looked as fit, as honed, as lethal, as ever. And her fingers practically itched to reach out and test it for herself.

Discreetly, she moved her arms behind her back and balled her fists into each other.

And then, finally, she let her gaze travel lower. Down the snug, black motorcycle leathers, which did little to disguise impossibly muscular thighs, and down…

She froze.

For a moment, the fluttering receded as a wave of nausea threatened to close over her head. She couldn't tear her gaze away, couldn't even breathe. Like a swimmer caught in a riptide, fighting to stay focussed and keep their head above the surface.

What had he been saying? Asking her?
Think. Think!

Slowly, so slowly, her brain kicked back into gear. Something about her being back…?

Her tongue took a moment to work loose again.

'It's true,' she confirmed stiffly.

And perhaps needlessly. After all, it was self-evident, wasn't it? Or maybe Zeke was simply giving her the opportunity to rethink her decision and get out of there. Out of Delburn Bay. Out of his corner of the country. Out of his life.

Just as she'd done the last time he'd commanded it.

And if it weren't for Seth, then maybe she would have done just that.

'Although, I'd hardly say I'm back.' She licked her dry lips even as she silently berated herself for such an outward show of nervousness. 'I'm far enough up the coast from Westlake.'

'I think you can call that *back*—' his voice was like a hot cocoa river running through her, and warming her, even as she tried to fight it '—given that it's the closest you've been to *coming home* in around fifteen years.'

Coming home. It sounded so…easy, when dropped from Zeke's lips, and suddenly the realisation terrified her. It meant that home wasn't Westlake where she'd grown up, or Delburn Bay where her father had moved to. Home was where Seth was.

But it was also where Zeke was.

And that absolutely, positively, was not acceptable.

'I disagree,' she lied, aware that folding her arms across her chest was a defensive, negative gesture, yet wholly unable to stop herself.

'No, you don't. You might be here, but you desperately wanted to come all the way to Westlake. You just couldn't bring yourself. It's obvious. You were never very good at lying to me, Tia.'

God, she'd made a monumental mistake coming back here.

It was too soon. She wasn't ready.

'I'm not lying,' she lied, desperation reverberating through every syllable.

Zeke's mouth curled up at one corner, making it seem as if that were actually a bad thing. But she had to concede that he had a point. Which only made it all the more ironic that he'd never realised she'd told him the biggest lie of all.

Before she could answer, he moved into the room—or maybe *prowled* was more accurate—and she couldn't drag her gaze away for even a second. Every bit the most virile, red-blooded, lethally powerful man she'd ever known. Something fluttered low in her belly, like a thousand butterflies all taking flight at once.

She couldn't still want him, still *ache* for him, after all this time. Surely? It was ridiculous. Unconscionable. She couldn't allow it.

She *wouldn't*.

'Then why Delburn Bay, Tia?'

Was she really ready to answer that?

Anyway, *Tia* was the naïve fifteen-year-old girl who had fallen for the handsome, charismatic seventeen-year-old boy the moment they'd volunteered together at Westlake lifeboat station a lifetime ago. *Tia* was the twenty-eight-year-old whose life had changed in a single instant and everything had been turned on its head.

She hadn't been *Tia* for five years.

'It's Antonia now.'

Whether she'd intended it as a distraction or a feeble attempt to take control of the situation, she couldn't be sure. Either way, it fell about as heavily as an anchor on a freight ship.

'The truth, *Tia*,' he pressed her, with deliberate emphasis.

The truth was something she wasn't ready for. But, just like that, just because Zeke had spoken, she was *Tia* again. As though the last five years had never happened.

'How did you know I was here?'

'The lifeboat community is tight-knit. People talk. You should know that.'

She ignored the voice in the back of her head whispering that was precisely why she'd come to Delburn Bay. She'd banked on that same tight-knit community to relay the news to Zeke that she *had* returned.

Just…not so unbelievably quickly.

'Did my father tell you I was here?'

The bark of laughter—if that was what it could be called—was less amused and more incredulous.

'Your father?'

'I'm staying with him. At least, until I find a place of my own.'

'And here I was thinking you were as much *persona non grata* as I am. The man who warned you that I couldn't love you, that I didn't even know what love was, and that we'd never last. Did you tell him you were only too happy to leave, or does he think it was all me?'

She had no idea whether he intended to wound her with the offhand remarks, or not. Probably the former. Then again, she deserved it, even if not for the reason Zeke could have known about. Another surge of guilt coursed through her.

She hadn't exactly been fair to Zeke when she'd reached out to her father—after several years of rebuffing his attempts at offering the proverbial olive branch to her—in order to make amends. Yet another complication of her own making that would, at some point, need resolving. But not today. Today there were more important concerns to address.

Such as, if it hadn't been her father who had contacted him, then Zeke wouldn't know about Seth. *Right?*

An image stole into her head and a wide smile leapt instantly to her lips. It was all she could do to stamp it out.

Her precious Seth.

The happy, funny, in-love-with-life four-year-old boy who *really* mattered in all this, and the one person she would give her life to protect.

Seth—the little boy who had deserved not to be born into the tumultuous aftermath of Zeke's black ops mission gone so harrowingly wrong, and her own part in what had happened that night.

Seth, who deserved to know his father now that Zeke had finally managed to find some peace.

But not yet. Not like this. Not dropping it on Zeke like some kind of bombshell. She had one chance to get this right. Her son deserved for her to get it right. Hell, even Zeke deserved for her to get it right. She would *not* blurt it out now like some kind of weapon against him. Hadn't she done them both enough harm already?

Her entire insides shook at the mere idea of it whilst his intense gaze, pinning her to the spot, seemed to confirm it.

Zeke stared at the ghost in front of him, not wanting to even blink in case she disappeared in that fleeting tenth of a second.

It was incredible.

How many times had he planned on tracking her down this past year? Now that he was finally on track. Now that he could be sure he wouldn't be a burden for her. Now that he finally had something to offer her again.

How Herculean it had been to resist that temptation. After all that had happened between them, and all that he'd said to her, he knew he had no right just to walk back into her life. He couldn't expect to pick back up where they'd left off.

But it hadn't stopped him imagining that maybe, just maybe, there would have been no one else for her but him. The way that there had never been—never would be—anyone else for him but Tia. *His* Tia.

He had no right to any of that. He'd lost that right five years ago when he'd sent her away, and then, when that hadn't worked, had said all those things to her in order to get her to leave him. Harsh, cruel words chosen for maximum wounding, for devastating effect. Words that made him blanch when he thought back to them, even now.

And yet a nonsensical part of him was still galled that she'd bought any of it. That she'd left.

Those five years felt like a lifetime ago, now. So much had changed. *He* had changed. He had healed, mentally and physically, and he had moved on with his life. But he'd never moved on from Tia. He'd carried her with him this whole time, like his private talisman, even her memory enough to galvanise him into action, to try to walk, on days when he might otherwise have curled up in a ball and imagined dying on his black ops mission that fateful night.

Just as two of his buddies had.

Every time he'd wondered why he was still here when they weren't, whether he deserved to still be here when they weren't, he'd thought of Tia, and known he had to try.

Which was why, when he'd finally turned his life around several years ago, he'd come back to Westlake, where they'd first met as kids. A foolish part of him hoping that somehow it would get back to her that he was here. A selfish part of him imagining that she might turn up, on whatever pretext she liked, just to see him.

He'd never really expected it to happen, and yet now here she was. Looking as glorious, as tempting, as *Tia*, as ever.

It was all he could do not to cross the space between them and haul her to him. To hold her and prove he wasn't simply imagining it.

'You look…well,' she faltered and flushed, her eyes skimming straight down his legs. 'Better than well.'

Had he really been so simple-minded to think she would look at him again without seeing... that?

He wasn't prepared for the familiar pain that

shattered through him. A pain he'd thought he had finally beaten into submission eighteen months ago, but which eighteen minutes in this one woman's company seemed to have resurrected with brutal efficiency.

It took all he had not to reach down the leg of his leather biker gear and feel for the lower limb that was no longer there.

That hadn't been there since Tia had cut it off five years and two months ago.

'Are you saying that to make me feel better?' he growled. 'Or you?'

'Zeke… I'm sorry,' she choked out, taking a few stumbling steps towards him. 'You have no idea how sorry.'

'Stop.' His hand flew up, halting both her advice and her words. And his own voice was harsh, razor-sharp even to his own ears. 'I don't want to hear it.'

Not least because she wasn't the one who should be doing any apologising. She shouldn't be sorry for what had happened on that makeshift operating table; she'd carried out the only option left to her. And in doing so, she had saved his life.

The fact that he'd accused her of ruining it meant that any apologies were his to make. He was the one who had pushed her away. She hadn't simply walked out on him, or cast him off faster than a Special Forces wannabe dropped his fifty-pound rucksack after his first fifteen-mile tab. He'd pushed her away. Hard. And without any show of mercy.

His only consolation had been the fact that it was the only way he could save her from feeling guilty or responsible every time she looked at him. The only way he could release her from being burdened with him.

But that had been five years ago, and a lot had changed since then. *He* had changed. How many times had he imagined finding her? Explaining himself to her? But not here, not like this. He needed to do it properly. To show her how he'd turned his life around.

This was the chance he'd been waiting for to get her back. And he wasn't about to blow it.

If only he could work his tongue loose to say a damned word.

'I heard you've been awarded a medal for bravery,' Tia blurted out, clearly unable to stand the silence any longer. 'For saving three crewmen from a sinking ship in heavy seas.'

'I was doing my job.' He could feel himself scowling even as he tried to stop it.

'The newspapers don't seem to think so,' she babbled on but, irrationally, he was more fascinated by the way her pulse was leaping erratically at her throat. 'They're calling you a hero.'

He'd hated the publicity for that. The *hero* nonsense. The public had lauded him for that lifeboat rescue, yet all he could think was that they didn't even know the names of the buddies he'd served with, who had died that night five years ago trying to protect their freedom.

'I think they're right,' she concluded almost shyly, giving him an unexpected flashback to the day his chip-on-the-shoulder seventeen-year-old self had first met the blushing fifteen-year-old he'd had no idea would change his life so dramatically.

He clenched his fists behind his back and fought the unnerving impulse to stride across the room and close that gap between them.

And then what...kiss her? It made no sense. A confusion of questions crowded his brain, screaming for his attention. He fought against the ear-splitting ringing in his head. Strident. Throbbing.

What had he been thinking, coming here? Leaping on his motorbike and hurtling up the stretch of coast from Westlake to Delburn Bay the moment he'd heard she was here?

Like a lovesick teenager, worshipping at her altar. All these...*emotions,* jostling and tumbling inside him. And he had no idea what to do with them all. But then, he always had lost his head when it came to Tia, ever since he'd given into temptation and kissed her on her sixteenth birthday.

Even now he could still remember every detail as they'd stood on the beach, the moonlight glistening off the inky water whilst her party had been in full flow in the beach house a few hundred metres away. A party that he hadn't been invited to because, let's face it, no one nice ever invited his family anywhere, and who could blame them for not wanting any one of four boys dragged up by an alcoholic, aggressive, abusive father?

But Tia had been different.

She'd looked *at* him, rather than *down on* him. She'd told him he was nothing like them, that he was one of the best lifeguards she'd ever seen. And he'd basked in the novelty of her admiration.

The night of her birthday she'd seen him on the beach, pretending not to stare in at everyone else having fun, and she'd come to demand her birthday gift from him. When he'd told her he didn't have one, she'd simply shrugged her shoulders and told him, *Of course you do.*

And then she'd stepped forward, pressing the entire length of her body against his, and she'd lifted her head and kissed him. In that instant she'd found a way past all his armour. Past every single one of the barriers that he'd been erecting for as long as he could remember.

He'd vowed, right there and then, to never let her go. And he wouldn't have…if it hadn't been for that night.

And now she was back. But was she here because she knew he was in Westlake, or had she just moved to be closer to her father?

Or someone else?

The unwanted thought slid through him. What if Tia had moved on? It made him answer more curtly than he had intended.

'I don't give a damn what the newspapers say.'

She licked her lips.

'No… I…don't suppose you do. You never did care what anyone thought.'

He had cared what *she* thought. His Tia. He cared that she was here. And he wanted her back in his life.

But this wasn't how he'd intended to do it. *Any* of it. He'd imagined that if Tia ever returned to his life, he would apologise to her. He would take her to the house he'd built on the plot of land by the Westlake lighthouse—just as their teenage selves had imagined one day doing together—and he would find a way to sit her down and explain what had happened five years ago. To finally find a way to open up to her.

Maybe even to win her back. In time. If he took things slowly enough.

Instead, he'd heard she was here and he'd simply reacted, jumping on his bike and racing up here. He had no idea what to say, or how to start. He could hardly expect her to just jump on the back of his bike, as she'd used to, and let him take her back to Westlake.

He was handling this all wrong. But far from the smooth reunion of his fantasies, *this* reunion was unravelling faster than a ball of para cord dropped down a knife-edge mountainside.

A fist of anger thrust its way back to the forefront of his brain. At himself more than at Tia. Yet still Zeke grabbed at it; he welcomed it. He could deal with *that* emotion far better than this unfamiliar blind panic that threatened to engulf him.

'Anyway,' she was still prattling on unhappily, 'it was impressive, what you did that night. You—'

'Why are you really here, Tia?'

He interrupted her abruptly, his question deliberately curt and jagged, zipping through the air like the verbal equivalent of a Japanese throwing star. He needed to understand what had brought her back; only then could he formulate his best tactical approach.

She blinked and fell silent for a moment.

'My job,' she offered shakily.

'So I heard. Apparently, you're back here as a medical officer for this lifeboat station. What about your career as an army doctor? Does that not appeal to you any longer?'

'I left the army. I'm starting as a locum at the nearby hospital next month, about the same time I officially start volunteering here. I came back because…well, because… I had to.'

She lifted her shoulders helplessly, but the action also caused her chest to rise and fall, the luscious curve of breasts with which he had once been so intimately acquainted snagged his gaze and, for a long moment, he couldn't drag his gaze away.

The hazy cloud of lust was infiltrating him all over. Slipping past his defences as though they were made of mere gauze.

'So you aren't an army doctor any longer. You quit?'

'It's…complicated.'

'That's pathetic.' He snorted, hating the way she was guarded with him even as he understood exactly why she was. 'Even *you* can do better than that, Tia.'

She blinked as though she wasn't quite sure how to answer. Then, abruptly, she straightened her back and tilted her chin into the air. So Tia-like.

'I'm back because I love lifeboats. You seem to forget that I was volunteering down here ever since I was a young teenager. Long before your seventeen-year-old backside came bouncing into town to become a beach lifeguard. Becoming a volunteer medical officer is only following in my father's footsteps. It's how he met my mother—'

She stopped abruptly and he had no idea how he resisted the impulse to go to her.

He knew only too well how Tia's parents had met. He hadn't been around at that time but it was well documented in the lifeboat community, and he'd heard the story often enough. Though never from Tia herself.

Her father had been a medical officer, her mother a coxswain. For twenty years they had volunteered alongside each other, right up until the fateful night when Celia Farringdale had been called out to a shout in heavy seas.

A trawler had lost engines several miles out. Celia's crew had attended, assisting the rescue helicopter to winch to safety all eight men from the stricken vessel, three of whom had been seriously injured. The helicopter had made three trips over several hours, with the lifeboat waiting, protecting, in case they had needed to abandon ship. Just as the last man had been pulled aboard the heli and it had turned for shore, the sea had swelled and crashed causing the lifeboat to roll unpredictably—just as the trawler had been lifted out of the water only to slam down onto the lifeboat's bow. Instantaneous and fatal. None of the lifeboat crew had survived.

Tia had been fourteen. The year before he'd met her for the first time. A kid who had tried so hard to be strong, and untouched by her past, and invincible.

In many ways seeing her had been like holding a mirror up to his own soul.

Was that why now, with emotions playing across her features however much she tried to fight them, Zeke felt like a heel? Enough to make his determination to take things slowly wane for a moment. Enough to let an altogether more welcome sensation invade his body.

Desire.

When refusing to acknowledge it didn't work, he imagined crushing it under the unforgiving sole of his boots.

'I know you have a tie to this place. Your family

was part of this community since before you or I were even born,' he offered by way of apology.

She actually gritted her teeth at him.

'I'm not trying to play *who has the greater claim*, Zeke. I'm just saying that…it's understandable why I want to be here.'

She was holding something back; he knew her well enough to be able to tell. But neither could he deny the point she was making. But whatever else either of them might say was curtailed by the sound of movement outside. Clearly an incident was going down.

'So that's why you're back?'

The hesitation was brief. *Blink and you'd miss it.*

'Yes.'

He couldn't explain why it crept through him as it did.

Was she back for someone else?

But then there was the sound of footsteps and he knew that someone was coming down the corridor. Maybe for Tia.

He'd waited five years for a conversation he'd never been sure would ever take place—and now it was about to be interrupted. Exactly as he'd feared.

Frustration swamped him, making his words

harsher, his voice edgier, than he'd intended them to be.

'I don't know, Tia. Maybe I thought you'd returned because you'd read about me in the papers and finally remembered that you were still my *wife*.'

CHAPTER TWO

TIA HURRIED DOWN the hallway, the emergency somehow grounding her.

She'd never been so happy for an interruption as she had been when one of the lifeguards had knocked on the door to tell her that they were dragging a struggling dog walker out of the surf and she might be needed.

Technically, she hadn't started yet but, until they knew what it was or whether the emergency services would need to be called, she could certainly take a look.

The confrontation with Zeke had been harder, so much harder, than she'd imagined it would be. He'd brought her to her knees with just a few curt words. So any further, awkward conversations with Zeke could—mercifully—wait.

Turning the corner, Tia spotted one of the lifeguards guiding a disorientated-looking woman up the steps, a dog leaping around behind them. The woman was moving under her own steam but looked weak.

'This is Marie,' the lifeguard was saying as they approached. 'About forty minutes ago she was walking her dog when it ran into the water a bit too far and got into difficulties. She went into the water to rescue it but got a bit stuck herself so we ran in. We brought her back here for a warm drink and change of clothes and then she seemed okay. Then about five minutes ago, she started to take a turn.'

'So she wasn't this disorientated when you pulled her out?'

'No,' the lifeguard replied. 'She complained of feeling faint about ten minutes later but nothing more. This has got progressively worse since she's been here.'

Tia watched as Zeke moved quickly to the fainting woman's other side, putting her arm around his shoulders.

'She's going to go, Billy,' he warned. 'Put your hand under her thigh and we'll carry her through. Quickly.'

The two men had barely got her to the consulting bed when she stopped breathing.

'Zeke, get her on the bed and get me a defib. Billy—' Tia turned to the lifeguard as he was dropping the woman's rucksack and coat from his shoulder '—call treble nine.'

'Heart attack?' Zeke asked, yanking the cupboard open and producing the defibrillator that Tia hadn't yet had a chance to locate.

'Could be.' Tia ripped open a mechanical ventilating kit and began to administer oxygen to help the woman start breathing again. 'But it may be drug related. Her skin is clammy and I don't like that purple colour.'

'Look there, it's like a rash,' Zeke noted, peering at the woman's arm.

Tia nodded, but her attention turned straight back to her casualty as she saw the woman begin to blink.

'Marie? Marie, are you with me? Good girl. Okay, my name is Tia, I'm a doctor. Have you got any medical conditions?'

'Where's Badge?'

'Is Badge your dog?' Tia guessed, as the woman nodded. 'Badge is fine, he's with our lifeguards now, probably being spoiled rotten.'

As she'd hoped, Marie began to relax.

'So, do you have any medical conditions?'

'None.' She shook her head as best she could with the ventilating mask still over her mouth and nose.

'Has anything like this ever happened to you before?'

Again, Marie shook her head.

'What about this rash?' Tia asked, as Zeke gently lifted the woman's arm to show her.

'Yeah, I get that on my arms or feet sometimes when I've been walking the dog here. It feels itchy and swollen.'

'When you go in the water?' Tia asked, her mind racing.

'I guess. But it goes pretty quickly usually.'

'Okay, I think we might need to run a few tests. An ambulance should be arriving fairly quickly to get you checked out at hospital.'

'Badge...?'

'Is there anyone we can call to get him picked up? He can stay here with us until they get here.'

'My dad. But you really think I need to go to hospital?'

'I suspect you might be suffering from cold urticaria, where your skin has a reaction either to the cold, or to cold water. Given that this is your first serious reaction, I'm guessing it was triggered by plunging into the sea after your dog. Technically, it was most likely the warming phase when you got here and changed clothes. But you do need to get checked out.'

The sound of the ambulance siren reached Tia's ears.

'Zeke...'

'I'll go and bring them,' he pre-empted, already heading out of the door and leaving her alone with her thoughts, which would no doubt be banging down the proverbial door once her patient was safely handed over to the ambulance crew.

Such as the fact that they had fallen into working together with such ease, despite their earlier confrontation.

And the fact that—aside from the reality that he had sought her out first—she had actually returned to the area with the intention of finding Zeke and finally being able to tell him that he had a son.

So far, she had done neither.

'Don't think our earlier conversation is over, Tia,' he warned softly as they turned away from the ambulance. 'You aren't running away from me this time.'

'I thought I heard Albert mention that you're due on call tonight, at Westlake. That's a ninety-minute drive from here.'

'Don't test me, Tia.' Her skin goosebumped at his grim tone. 'You might have thought Delburn Bay was far enough away from Westlake that I wouldn't know you were here, but you should have known better. And I still want to talk to you.'

She forced herself to meet his eye. She could do this. For Seth.

'And I need to talk to you, too,' she echoed. 'Properly. Like the adults we now are, instead of somehow regressing to those naïve, idealistic, opinionated kids we once were.'

'Is that so?'

If her heart hadn't been lodged somewhere in her throat, the threads of her thoughts threatening to unravel at any moment, she might have laughed at the surprise on his face.

She knew what was coming, and yet somehow she was still here. Still breathing. In and out. In and out.

Not running away this time.

'It is so,' she confirmed at length. 'Zeke, for what it's worth, I'm sorry.'

If she'd kicked him in the guts she didn't think he could look more shocked.

'You have nothing, *nothing*, to be sorry about,' he ground out.

God, if only that were true.

Where did she even start? Her mind spun as she hurried through the lifeboat station and back to her soon-to-be office, needing just a moment alone to compose herself.

As if she hadn't had five years.

As if meeting Zeke, and telling the truth,

hadn't been one of the main reasons she'd come so close to home. To finally tell him about her son—*their* son—because it was the right thing to do.

However terrified she might be.

And then they were back in her office, the door closed, and the rest of the world shut out. Tia crossed to the desk, not turning around until she was on the other side of it, using it like some kind of defensive barrier, not that Zeke appeared to have any intention of coming any nearer to her anyway.

They met each other's gaze for a few moments—maybe an eternity—neither of them wanting to be the first to break the silence.

But one of them was going to have to, and, after everything, Tia knew it had to be her. She owed him that much.

'You've changed,' she managed.

'You already said that.' He scowled. 'I believe your words were that I look *better than well*.'

'Right,' she muttered, shaking her head lightly, almost imperceptibly. But he did look well. And changed. Beyond all recognition.

Oh, not in the physical way, of course. Now that the initial shock of their first encounter was behind her, that much was evident. But in terms of the broken man he'd been when she'd last seen and spoken to him. The bleak, black pit he had been in back then. The pit into which—a part of her had never been able to shake the feeling—she'd helped to push him.

Tia's heart pounded so hard in her chest that she was half surprised it didn't batter its way out. Because the truth was that she didn't know Zeke any better than she had as a naïve, adoring kid. This reunion was so much more unpleasant than anything she had feared.

And with what she was about to tell him, it was about to get that much worse.

The storm that raged through Zeke was so much more powerful than that force ten gale that had been blowing all day at sea, so destructive that it threatened to rip him apart. To tear down every last piece of his once broken self that it had taken almost half a decade to put back together.

This wasn't anything like he'd expected today to go.

Meeting Tia again had completely, unexpectedly, unbalanced him. For the last three years he'd been slowly starting to feel more human again. More real. Yet one conversation with Tia and she'd seen through him in an instant.

Without a word she seemed to call him out for being the sham that he was.

He could feel the ground rolling beneath him like the treacherous, shifting sands that lay further out from the bay. Something else roiled inside him. Hope? Uncertainty? Both?

Without warning, the burning, twisting, phantom limb pain that hadn't troubled him for years now threatened to rear itself again. It took everything he had not to reach his hand down and touch his leg.

Where his past met his present. Innocence and reality. Destructible human flesh and the bionics of the future.

He truly was a million-dollar man these days. In more ways than one. A man with whom plenty of women were only too eager to be. But not a single one of them could ever have hoped to come close to the incomparable Antonia Farringdale.

Which was why he'd never bothered with anyone else. Not once.

It was why he was determined to win her back. But he couldn't give her the satisfaction of knowing she had that kind of advantage over him. He wouldn't.

Pushing the phantom pain back, Zeke held eye contact and stared her down. It was all in his head. A mere manifestation of all that he had lost—so much more than just the leg itself—the night what remained of his black ops team had flown him into the single-man makeshift clinic in the middle of no man's land.

And his white-faced wife had been given no choice but to perform an emergency amputation on him.

'So, are the newspapers the real reason you're back? You read about my so-called heroics?'

He hated saying the words; he'd never much cared for public veneration. Not as a young seventeen-year-old lifeguard who had just happened to be on the beach when the mayor's daughter had got caught out by a riptide. Not as a twenty-something decorated marine when he'd made it out of that mission with a limb missing but alive, when two of his buddies had been brought out in body bags. And not in this latest award, as a coxswain who'd just happened to get lucky on a horrible, stormy night.

And yet, as he watched the battle waging within Tia as she fought to keep her cool in the face of his outrageous accusations, a little punch of victory vibrated through his bones. As pathetic as it might be that he took such triumph from the fact that he could still read her, he would take whatever he could right at this moment.

Because little else about her seemed the same. At least, not when he got past the physical similarities. Those brown eyes with the flecks of green, that light brown hair now highlighted with pure gold, that body that made his whole body tighten and his mouth water.

'You heard I was here, and you couldn't stop yourself from racing home to be with me again?' he pushed on, not missing the way her nostrils flared. As though he wasn't entirely wrong and she hated herself for it.

And if that was true, then surely it meant she still felt something for him?

There was still hope.

'I see you aren't denying it.' He grinned, enjoying the way her eyes sparked with anger.

'Denying what?' she challenged. 'Denying wanting to appear in the newspapers with you as your desperate ex-wife?'

'Not ex,' he gritted out. 'We're still married.'

'Fine.' She exhaled deeply, but her voice was that bit tighter, thicker than before. 'Estranged for the last five years, then. Either way, I'm confused.'

'And why is that?'

'Well, let's see.' She lifted her hand as though to tick off her points one at a time. 'First you say I'm in Delburn Bay because I thought it was far enough from Westlake for you not to know I was here. Then you declare that I've come because

I've read the papers and wanted a piece of your new-found fame. So which is it to be, Zeke? Because even you can't have it both ways.'

It was that flash of temper, her refusal to cower, which he had fallen in love with all those years ago. And which clawed their way inside him right now. It made him want to pull her to him when he knew he should be taking things slowly.

But it was proving impossible to hold back when she had essentially returned to him after so many years of absence. Especially when she looked at him the way she was doing right now, even if he doubted she realised it. As if she still wanted him, too.

'You didn't answer my question,' he pointed out smoothly.

Tia merely cocked an eyebrow.

'Fancy that.'

The need to claim her as his once more swirled inside him, pounding at him, eroding him. His arms actually ached with the effort of not reaching out to touch her. To place his hands on her shoulders and draw her in. To see if her body still fitted his with as flawlessly as ever. To discover if she was every bit the Tia he remembered.

Would she think he was still the same Zeke who she had married over fifteen years ago? She was certainly the same Tia. Despite that…edge, which he couldn't quite pinpoint.

'You haven't changed,' he told her, taking a step closer.

Unable to stop himself.

She braced herself, though he noted she didn't try to move away.

'Don't, Zeke. I have changed, as it happens.' And again, something shot through him too fast for him to grasp. 'More than you can imagine. As, I've no doubt, have you.'

Zeke faltered for a moment, then caught himself. She couldn't be back for the money. Tia couldn't know that he was now a multimillionaire thanks to his company, Z-Black, along with Zane—another of his former marine brothers-in-arms—and Zane's investment mogul brother, Frazer.

He took another step towards her.

'Meaning?'

This time, she did edge away, if only a fraction. And as though her body didn't want to but her head was telling her she had to. She squeezed her eyes shut.

'Meaning, you can't drop me, like you did, and now pick me back up again and expect me to just fall into your arms.'

'I didn't *drop* you.'

'As good as,' she argued shakily. 'We were meant to be partners, Zeke. Husband and wife. But you pushed me away. You didn't trust me.'

He resisted the urge to squeeze his eyes shut; it only made the memories all the more vivid. Real. Even now, very occasionally, he would still wake up in a sweat, reliving that final mission. A mission that had gone south so quickly that his team had had no chance to extract themselves.

The torpedo. The explosion. Then blood in the water all around him, just before everything had gone black. He hadn't even felt the pain at that point.

'I lost everything that night,' he growled, abruptly.

'Yes.' Tia tilted her head up determinedly and met his gaze for the very first time. 'And so did I.'

'Don't go there, Tia.'

Anyone else would have heeded the warning note in his voice. Tia merely swallowed hard, but she stood her ground.

'Why not? Because only you get to own that pain? You don't think I carried it, too?'

'Why do you think I told you to leave?' he bit out. This was insane. It wasn't how he'd imagined things going in any version of meeting up with Tia again. 'I wanted you to be free of it. I released you so that you could walk away and never look back. I've carried it with me for these past five years so that you didn't have to.'

'And yet I have,' she matched him, her eyes shimmering unexpectedly.

Deep within him alarm bells rang, but he couldn't heed them. Couldn't stop himself.

'What? What have you carried, Tia?'

She stopped. Glowering. Emotions charging all over her face. And then, just as suddenly as her temper had flared, she reined it in. The loss was unbearable. He felt her withdrawing and he had no idea how to stop it from happening.

It hurt. Far more than it had any right to.

'I'm sorry,' she choked out, as though she knew how his chest was tightening excruciatingly.

Zeke didn't realise he'd crossed the room to her until she tilted her head to look up at him, her eyes growing darker, her mouth opening just a fraction, her breathing quickening.

And still, Zeke didn't stop himself.

'This can't be why you came home, Tia. It certainly isn't why I drove up here tonight.'

His voice was huskier than it had any right to be. He needed to leave. Now. Tia needed space to think, and he needed to get out of there before he broke all his rules about taking things slowly if they were to stand a chance of piecing their relationship back together.

So why, instead of moving away, was he reaching to take her chin in his fingers, his entire body revelling in the way her breath caught sharply?

CHAPTER THREE

THE URGE TO kiss her pressed in all around Zeke.

He leaned in closer. So close that he could feel her warm breath brushing over his skin. The energy waves bouncing off her and onto him made his entire body goosebump in anticipation.

The whole world had fallen away, and he could see no one—nothing—else, but Tia.

'It's been too long,' he murmured.

She lifted her hands to his sides, then a tiny frown settled over her forehead.

'Your T-shirt's wet.'

'It's from carrying that woman's stuff. It was soaking.'

He felt so on fire right at that moment that it had barely registered.

'It's cold.' Tia sounded concerned, but he couldn't have cared less.

'It's just a T-shirt. You're stalling. But there's nothing to be nervous about. It's just me.'

He dipped his head again.

'Please.' Her voice was a fragile whisper. 'Don't do this, Zeke.'

A token protestation at best.

'Tell me you don't want me to kiss you,' he murmured, his lips closing the gap to hers.

'I...' The sound might as well have been ripped from her throat. And she still didn't move. 'I can't.'

And then, as if suddenly galvanised into action, Tia stumbled backwards. Away from him.

He was an idiot.

He'd frightened her off. Exactly as he'd cautioned himself not to do.

'You can't just expect...' she prattled on. 'I mean...after five years...things have changed.'

'But not the way you feel about me,' he countered smoothly.

She eyed him balefully.

'You're wrong. The way I feel about you *has* changed.'

'Mmm...' He wasn't in the least perturbed. 'You say that, but your body is telling me something quite different.'

'My body evidently doesn't know when to shut up, then,' she snapped.

But her tone was that little bit more brittle than he might have expected. As though there was something he was missing.

Tia raked her hands through her hair in a gesture he recognised only too easily as an indicator of just how wound up she was.

'I can't just fall back into your arms, Zeke. I won't. You don't understand. I... There are things I need to tell you.'

'More apologies for amputating my leg?' he countered. 'I don't need to hear them.'

Moreover, he didn't want to hear them. Especially after all he'd put her through.

And then, suddenly, she seemed to gather herself together and straighten her shoulders.

'I'm not apologising for amputating your damn leg,' she burst out. 'I didn't come back here for that. And I didn't come back here for us. I've moved on, Zeke. Just like you told me to do.'

'If I truly believed that, I would walk away,' he stated flatly, ignoring the way every fibre of his body ignited in protest. 'But I can still read you, Tia. I know you want me.'

She bit her lip but she didn't deny it. He'd known she wouldn't.

'Fine. So, what, then? Do you expect me to put your abrupt return to the area down to curiosity? You've already admitted you read about me in the papers, and knew I was back in Westlake. And suddenly, you're back here. A mere ninety minutes up the coast. And don't tell me it's because your father is here in Delburn, because he has been here for several years now and you haven't been back before.'

'How do you know that?' retorted Tia, giving away more than she intended to.

'Because I've been back at Westlake for the last three years and you haven't been anywhere near the place.'

Without warning, Tia went white. He started forward, concerned she was about to faint, then checked himself as she stared him down. But it was the sheer misery on her face that really got to him.

'You've been here?' she breathed. 'For the past three years? When I read the article in the paper, it never mentioned how long you'd been here.'

'Westlake lifeboats offered me a position as coxswain when they heard I'd left the military,' he ground out, realising too late that he might have given himself away by his unintentional admission. 'I needed the job.'

'You said you would never come back here. Ever. You swore it. I read that article in the paper but I never dreamed you'd been here that long.'

'My God, Tia, I was a twenty-year-old kid when I made that stupid vow.'

She didn't need to know that the first thing he'd done when he'd straightened his life back out had been to return to Westlake—the place he'd abhorred as a kid—in the hope that Tia might also return home.

'Does it really surprise you that I'm not that broken, damaged, defeated, shadow of a man you thought I was?'

He ignored the part of him that wondered if she'd been entirely wrong in that conclusion. The part of him that wondered if he would ever get over the guilt he felt that he was still alive when members of his squad—his best buddies—were gone.

Was it something he would *ever* get used to?

'No, it's just. I didn't know. I never imagined...' She shook her head. 'The point is, I didn't come here to revisit old history.'

'Well, you didn't come back just to make amends with your father,' he carried on grimly, as if it could distract her. 'Up until five years ago we were still a happily married couple and I know that in a decade of marriage you never once took up his olive branches.'

He couldn't be exactly sure what it was that he'd said, but suddenly her face grew harder. More determined. Another spark of the feisty Tia.

'Is this the game we're playing, then, Zeke?

You're rewriting history? Claiming that we were a happily married couple?'

Her voice swirled around the room, around him. Shaky, low yet unexpectedly dangerous.

'Weren't we?'

'Constant deployments meant that we rarely spent longer than a week together at a time. So it always felt as though it was fresh, and thrilling, and new. But we weren't a couple as most people would consider that to be. We didn't really share things, at least not our fears, or our flaws.'

'Do many couples?'

'The strongest do.' She shrugged. 'You and I were two kids running away from our pasts, if for different reasons. And whilst I never thought that that IED defeated you, if we're being fair you were damaged long before then.'

'Say again.' Less of a question, more of a challenge.

But to her credit, Tia didn't back down.

'The fact that you never let your childhood, that…monster who called himself your father, break you was one of the qualities which made you the kind of loyal, dedicated marine who everyone wanted on their squad.'

It was sad how much he actually *ached* to believe her.

He nearly did.

Instead, he began a long, slow clap.

'Impressive. Have you been preparing that little show for a while, Tia? You almost had me convinced.'

'But, of course, I didn't,' she threw back without missing a beat. So fiery, so steadfast—the girl he had fallen in love with. 'Because you won't believe me no matter what I say. You never would. You decided what was true for yourself, and anyone else's opinion be damned.'

'I trusted you, too. Once,' he countered pointedly.

'No.' She shook her head. 'You didn't. You were so used to having to rely on yourself, knowing that no one else out there would look out for you, that you found it difficult to let me in.'

'But I did let you in.'

'No, you never did. Because when that last mission went wrong...' She faltered, then regrouped. 'When you ended up losing part of your leg, I was the last person you wanted. You pushed me away. Not just once, Zeke, but again and again.'

This was it. This was his opportunity to say all the things he'd been imagining telling her for half a decade. Instead, he found he couldn't. His head was all over the place, and things were unfolding in a way that didn't match any of the many and varied scenarios that he had envisaged.

He felt reactive. Quite different from the proactivity with which he was usually characterised. And suddenly he found himself falling back on the arguments he'd used back then. When he'd been angry, and desperate, and grieving for the life, the career, he'd had but would never have again. When the only thing he'd felt as though he'd been able to control had been stopping it from impacting on Tia's life too.

'It was for the best.'

'Not for me. Not back then.'

'You didn't need the burden of a cripple.'

'You still believe that's what you are?' she cried out.

'No, of course not.' He'd got past that long ago. The army rehab centre had made sure of it. Wallowing hadn't been an option; the centre had ensured the guys were all up at dawn, making their beds, carrying out daily ablutions, just as they'd all done years before in basic training. It had instilled the work ethic back in them, treating rehab like a training routine, like a job, and tea and sympathy had been far, far down the list.

It was what guys like him—ex-military—had needed. That discipline, those expectations, the rules, had been familiar and comforting.

'Forget I said that.' He hauled off his sodden, icy tee, furious with himself. 'I'm lucky. I got off lightly compared to so many guys.'

What was wrong with him? Why was he acting like the arrogant chip-on-the-shoulder kid he'd thought he'd left behind a long, long time ago?

'Do you still blame me for amputating?'

'Say again?' He stood up incredulously.

He had come to terms years ago with the fact that Tia hadn't had any choice. His role in black ops meant that only a handful of people would ever have known where he was. Tia's commanders would have had no idea that his squad were even within a hundred miles. And his commanders couldn't have changed *her* posting or it would have been a sign that they were planning a black ops mission.

Besides, there had been no reason at all to think that *that* particular mission ran any real risks. It had been a complete curveball to all of them.

But when the IED had gone off and the medevac had come in, her little hearts-and-minds field hospital had been the only one they could have hoped to get to. The fact that she had been the only doctor in that camp was just devastatingly misfortunate.

Then again, she had saved his upper leg, and

maybe even his life. If she hadn't amputated above his ankle when she had, then by the time he'd got to the UK he would probably have lost the knee as well. If he'd even survived the journey back, of course.

He knew that. He'd known it by the time he'd got out of physio at the UK hospital, eight months later. Which brought him right back to the question of why was he acting like a belligerent teenager now?

Was it because she was the only person in the world—other than his old man, and he didn't really count—who had made him feel…*less*?

Less of a person. Less of a husband. Less of a *man*. The nightmares he'd had back then—still now—certainly didn't help matters.

'Then why did you push me away?' she croaked out.

How was he supposed to answer that?

Balling up his tee, he stuffed it viciously into his motorbike rucksack and pulled out a clean, fresh one from another compartment, before turning around to face her again. He wasn't prepared for the way her eyes were locked onto him. Or the desire that burned within those darkened irises.

She wanted to know that he didn't blame her for amputating? That he had forgiven her. He could say something, he could try to explain, but he'd never been good with words. He'd always been more of an actions man.

So maybe actions would convince her now.

Deliberately, he crooked his mouth and dropped his arms, delaying pulling on his fresh tee. The sense of triumph swelled as her gaze didn't slide away, instead holding fast. Her pulse leaping a moment at her throat, those flushed patches high on her cheeks, her lips parting a fraction.

His entire body reacted in that very instant. Carnal and primitive.

The next thing Zeke knew he was striding back across the room, snaking one hand around the back of her neck, and hauling her willing mouth to his.

That *thing* that had always been between them—so bright, so electric—blasted back into life with a power that almost knocked him backwards. Making him feel truly alive again.

After all this time.

His mouth feasted on hers, greedily swallowing up her gentle moan of pleasure as she matched his kiss, stroke for stroke, depth for depth. His body exulted in the feel of her against him, her breasts splayed against his chest, her heat against his sex. And still the kiss went on.

For an eternity.

Or longer.

It was almost unconscionable when she stiffened suddenly, lifting her palms to his chest, exerting some pressure.

As unpalatable as it was, he made himself release her. She stumbled back, cast around wildly and fluttered around her desk.

'We can't do that,' she whispered. 'Or...at least...we shouldn't.'

As though she thought that the wooden workspace could somehow prove a barrier between them, but the fact that she was leaning on it, her hands pressing on it as though subconsciously testing how sturdy it might be, belied her words.

He took a step forward.

'Why shouldn't we? We both want it.'

'Because someone might walk in.' Her ponytail bounced from side to side in agitation, though her lack of denial spoke louder than anything.

He'd always got a kick out of that catch in her voice. Desire laced with a need to at least *appear* to be responsible.

'Then we'll close the blinds.' He twisted the handle with a couple of deft flicks of his wrist.

Her breathing became a fraction shallower.

'Then we hang the sign on the door.' He flipped around the sign that warned people:

Medical Examination in Progress—Do Not Disturb. 'And finally, we lock the door.'

'It…it doesn't have a lock.' She swallowed hard.

Zeke glanced around, spotted the hard-backed dining chair from the rec room and, spinning it around with one hand, wedged it under the door handle.

'Consider it locked.' He shrugged. 'Any other concerns, Tia?'

She didn't reply immediately, she simply stared at him with overly wide eyes from across the room.

He advanced on her, leisurely, no rush, giving her a chance to object even if he hoped she wouldn't.

'I told you, it's Antonia.' Her voice was thick, loaded. He recognised it only too well and it was like a stroke of her hand against the very hardest part of him.

'Tia,' he repeated easily.

But he didn't know if he was still challenging her, or merely trying to remind her of who she had once been.

Who *he* had once been to her.

Another step, then another. And still she didn't move. He might have thought she was rooted to the spot but for the faint twist of her body towards him. As though it knew what she wanted, even if her head didn't.

Or was pretending not to.

'Here's your chance, Tia,' he murmured, so close now he could have reached out and touched her.

He knew it was virtually killing her not to melt into him. Her desire was etched into every soft feature on her delicate face. Plus, he was barely staying in control himself. He ached to reach out and touch her with a need that was excruciating. The one thing he was gripping onto so tightly was the knowledge that it was even more excruciating for Tia.

Just as it deserved to be.

She flicked a tongue out over her lips, her voice little more than a whisper.

'My chance?'

'To step away,' he rasped.

The charged silence arced between them and still he steeled himself.

'I'm not moving,' she whispered, her voice cracking.

'No,' he agreed.

The undercurrent rolled. Slowly, almost imperceptibly, she lifted her shoulders to him. A silent plea for him to move.

He held his ground.

'Suddenly I find I want to be sure,' he ground out. 'If you want more, come and get it.'

'Zeke...'

Her eyes gazed at him, tortured. *Another victory,* he told himself, forcing his expression to remain neutral.

'Your choice. I don't want there to be any question about this, Tia.'

For a moment she didn't move but then slowly, seemingly painfully, she lifted her clenched fists off the desk and pushed herself backwards, if only half a step.

Zeke could feel himself teetering on the edge of the abyss, struggling to keep his footing even as he knew he was too far gone. The ground felt as though it were shifting beneath him, even though he knew it was merely in his head.

And then, incredibly, she stepped forwards again. Towards him. Unsteadily. As though her body was acting on its own orders rather than any executed by her brain. But the expression on her face was so painfully familiar it was as though he were igniting from the inside out.

As she finally moved in front of him, going toe to toe, the last of his control went up in spectacular flames.

What the hell was she thinking?

The question flitted briefly into Tia's mind, but

then Zeke pinned her against the wall, his deliciously hard body bearing on her with wicked heaviness, and everything liquefied.

The past few hours had been so charged, so heady, that she'd almost lost sense of herself. Thrown back into the past, yet still rooted in the present. It felt surreal.

The first kiss had been like coming home, Tia thought weakly, even as it made her entire body ignite at his touch. But this one had her as though her body was no longer under her own control, reacting to him on an utterly primal level, whilst her brain had no say whatsoever in the matter.

She was vaguely aware that she should object, but instead her hands were threading through his hair, her mouth tingling with every brutal pass of his tongue, her body exalting with the hard, altogether too familiar pressure of Zeke against her.

'Where the hell did you go?' he demanded hoarsely, as though he was barely able to drag his mouth from hers enough to ask. As though he hadn't intended to ask, but instead the words had been ripped from somewhere deep inside.

She didn't know how to respond other than to shake her head minutely and press her lips to his again. Words could only complicate things.

And ruin them.

She just wanted to revel in the kiss that was

still pounding through her, hammering along her veins, firing her up as though the last five years had never happened.

Something sloshed around her head, a thought perhaps, maybe a reminder—no, more than that, a *warning*—but she couldn't grasp it. She didn't even want to try that hard.

So instead she simply obeyed as he tilted her head this way and that, testing her, tasting her. He was gentle one moment, demanding the next, his tongue sliding against hers, driving her wild, making her respond every time. It had been too long.

Far too long.

She heard the desperate, needy sound that escaped her lips. She felt the way her fingers clung to him, almost biting into the solid biceps, which time had done nothing to diminish. She experienced the ache—the *yearning*—as it flowed down through her very core, turning everything hot. Molten. Releasing five years of pent-up frustration.

The more roughly he kissed her, the more she pushed back, as if seeing his offering and raising the stakes. It was a dangerous game. A thrilling game. One that she was helpless to stop. Her overriding thought—*need*—was to reacquaint herself with every plane and contour of his body. To make up for all these awful years apart.

Lifting her arms, Tia wrapped them around his neck, shuddering when he let his hands trail down her body with such control that she was certain he was only trying to torment her.

He started with her neck, the backs of his fingers skimming a line down from her jaw to her chest. Tracing the edge of her crisp white shirt right down to the first—perhaps prudishly high—button, then back up the other side, pressing one kiss, then another, and finally a third.

She opened her mouth to say something, anything, but found she couldn't. Her mind was too foggy. And there was the haunting fear that if she said the wrong thing she might break this unexpected spell.

And yet…somewhere…something needled her. Niggled at her.

What was she forgetting?

But then he let his hands wander down her back, dancing over her spine, her hips, until they were cupping her backside and she could do nothing but move with him and press tighter to him.

Heat against steel. Heady and exhilarating.

Just as it had always been with him.

No other man had ever had this effect on her.

Not before Zeke, and certainly not after. She'd never even tried. There had never been anyone like him. And that, she told herself, was the only explanation for why she responded to him as if she were a drowning woman and he were the only one who could throw her a lifeline.

She shifted against him urgently, revelling in the sensation of every inch of his sinfully hard body pressed so exquisitely against every inch of her. Exalting as she heard the unmistakable catch of his breathing. Then the hot, still slick feel of his mouth again as she matched his kisses stroke for stroke, urging him on without even a word.

Moving herself against him, until he was reaching for her shirt, making only the briefest attempt to undo the awkward, slippery pearls before cursing softly into her mouth and simply giving one efficient tug. They popped off naughtily, then skittered noisily, feverishly, across the hard floor.

And then Zeke was dropping his hand lazily down the valley between her breasts, his knuckles grazing each soft swell, his tongue teasing swirls over her sensitive skin. Again and again he let his tongue sweep over her, each time stopping short of the nipples that swelled, almost painfully, with the need for him to touch them.

In the dim distance, she could hear her soft

moans, her half-uttered pleas, but it was surreal.
Like an old dream that she had clung to for so
many years. An old memory.

Yes, it had been far, far too long.

And yet…

As her memory clicked over, Tia allowed instinct to kick in. She let her hands glide over
Zeke's shoulders, drawing something from their
strength, their familiarity. She traced her fingers
over the bunched shoulder blades and down the
muscled back. She cupped his hard backside just
as he had done with her.

And then she very slowly, very deliberately,
lifted her hips up to meet him. To press against
the hard evidence of his own desire. The way
they had done countless times, so many years
ago, drawing him in as though it was her who
was doing the seducing, not him.

Perhaps that was why he suddenly drew back
from her, breaking the kiss and leaving her almost bereft, her eyes flashing open, her hands
reaching to cup his cheeks only for him to catch
them, and draw them to his chest.

'Zeke…'

'No.' His rebuttal was harsh, ragged. 'My pace.
Not yours.'

'I didn't—'

'Stop talking, Tia. Just wait,' he commanded.

She didn't think she could have done anything but obey, just as before, even if she'd wanted to. But the truth was, there was a part of her that was only too happy to stop thinking, stop running, and do exactly what Zeke told her to do.

Then he stopped, his face so tantalisingly close to hers, his gaze holding hers wordlessly, his eyes almost black with desire. When he slid his hands to her waistband, unhooked the buttons and the delicious lick of the zip wound its way into her ears, she thrilled in anticipation.

His hand dropped between them; she could only gasp, her eyelids feeling suddenly heavy as he toyed with her skimpy underwear, which had been like her own private joke with herself.

'Somewhat incongruous with that preppy, oh-so-professional shirt, aren't they?' he accused, but she took a little comfort in the huskiness of his voice, which betrayed him.

'I guess I like to surprise.'

His mouth tautened to a grim line.

'As do I.'

It only dawned on her what he was doing when he dropped abruptly to his knees and pushed her tight suit skirt up to her hips. He intended to make her lose control whilst he held onto his. Hardly fair, or sporting.

'Wait…' she protested, trying to jerk away, but

her voice was flimsy at best and, besides, he was more than ready for her. 'That isn't...'

The words died on her lips as Zeke deftly hooked her scrap of lace to the side and anointed her with his mouth, pulling one leg over his shoulder to allow him complete access.

Tia cried out, helpless to do anything but lean back on the edge of her desk and thread her hands through his hair, uncharacteristically longer than she ever remembered. And then her mind stopped thinking anything as he feasted on her, paying homage to her as though he had fantasised about doing this again, for as long as she had.

Even though she knew that, of course, was il-logical.

But this wasn't the time for doubts. Not when Zeke was revering her with his hands, his lips, his tongue. Licking into her until her hips were moving of their own accord, dancing to Zeke's sensual, primal tune. His rumbles of approval thrumming through her sex, and making her cry out again and again, barely able to stifle the sounds.

His strokes became deeper and more urgent, as if he couldn't get enough of her, and then... Zeke did that *thing* to her that only he had ever known. A white-hot carnal heat seared through her in seconds, and it was all she could do to bite her lip from screaming out.

Colours danced and exploded as her body shuddered uncontrollably, propelling her inexorably to the edge of the world. Or maybe it was the edge of nothing. And Zeke just kept up his relentless pace, driving her along faster and faster, his hands cupping her bottom all the tighter, to prevent her from backing away. His savage mouth an exquisite weapon against her. Possessing her. Finally finding her again after all these years.

And then he drew the sensitive bud into his mouth and sucked. Hard.

Tia came apart. Spinning and spiralling, going higher and higher, lost inside such an intense pleasure, which only Zeke could have brought her to.

By the time she came back to herself, hastily tugging her skirt back down and pulling the two sides of her now buttonless white shirt together, Zeke was standing halfway across the room. Triumph mingling with an odd black expression, which she couldn't read. But it panicked her.

Her head snapped up as reality crashed in.
Seth!

An image of her—their—son popped into her

head. This wasn't how she had intended to tell Zeke. Not after what had just happened. She needed time to think. To reorder her thoughts. To work out how she was supposed to tell him now.

What had she just done?

'Happy now?' she threw at him, her mind still whirring. Racing to catch up. 'Pleased with yourself?'

'Very,' he drawled.

'Because you can still get me to...'

'Orgasm?' he supplied helpfully, but the hard smile didn't quite reach his eyes.

'Yes.' She flushed, telling herself to take deep breaths. 'That.'

'No need to act coy now. Or are you simply aggrieved that I've proved wrong your claim that you no longer have residual feelings for me?'

Zeke was going to be furious when he found out. And what did that say about her that she'd forgotten her son so comprehensively?

'It's...complicated,' she faltered as Zeke frowned.

'How disappointingly clichéd, Tia. I would have expected better from you.'

Anger rolled unexpectedly over her. Possibly more at herself than at Zeke. After all, he didn't know.

'This isn't a game,' she snapped.

His hard smile was more a baring of teeth than anything genuine.

'I don't see why not.'

'No.' She deliberately ignored the voice asking her whose fault that was. 'I imagine that you don't.'

'Then elucidate.'

'Not here.' Tia stalled. 'Especially not after… *this*. But it can't go any further, Zeke. That can't happen. I won't allow it.'

'You're right, it shouldn't have happened.' His tone scratched deep inside her. Gouging at her.

So matter-of-fact, so undaunted, that it made her feel dismissed and unwanted by him all over again. And it hurt more than it had any right to.

As much as she wanted—*needed*—to tell him about Seth, she couldn't. Not after this. Not now, anyway.

She needed time to recompose herself. A night. A couple of days at most.

'I have to go,' she muttered, grabbing her purse and car keys and pushing past him.

Both sick and relieved when he let her go.

Tia had no idea how she got home. One moment she was leaving the lifeboat station, shifting her car into gear and hurtling out of the car park. The next, she was pulling into her father's driveway, blinking away the tears that threatened to spill out over her cheeks the entire eight-minute drive. And as she hurried up to the house her heart lifted at the sight of Seth's face peering out of the window, and his elated grin as he blew her frantic kisses.

She couldn't get her key in the door fast enough as she heard him racing down the hallway, already babbling to her about his day with Grampy. What was it about the prospect of a squeezing hug from her son that promised to settle her churning stomach and the turmoil of the past few hours better than any antacid ever would?

The door was barely open before Seth was dragging her inside, a finger painting in one hand and a sticky piece of toast in the other.

'Look, Mummy, I drew you a tiger catopolly.'

'Wow.' Tia crouched down right there and scooped her son into her arms, inhaling deeply the comforting scent of his freshly washed hair. Right now, she couldn't bear to look in those suddenly too familiar grey-blue eyes. Instead, she smiled brightly and took the picture.

'A big cat tiger, huh?'

'No,' he chuckled. 'A tiger catopolly. They're really fuzzy and there are lots of them on Delburn Island.'

'Oh, that's right, Grampy was taking you on the beach walk today,' she realised, making a great show of admiring the scribbled drawing. 'So this must be a tiger moth caterpillar?'

'Yes,' Seth declared proudly, his eyes sparkling as much as ever, and making her heart constrict. 'A tiger *moth* catopolly.'

'Well, I think it's marvellous,' she declared, shoving any last thoughts of Zeke out of her head.

Reaching out, she began to close the front door when a foot wedged itself in the way.

A big, biker-booted foot.

She almost tipped backwards in her haste to stand up. Instinct making her send her curious son to his grandfather and closing the living room door behind them.

She hadn't even noticed him following her, let alone heard his bike. Yet there it was, parked right on the driveway as though he had every right to be there.

And Zeke, looming and furious, in the doorway. His eyes locked onto the closed door as she gripped the handle as though that could somehow delay the inevitable.

'What the hell, Tia?'

'Zeke...'

She should have told him. Back there in the

lifeboat station. It was why she'd come back to Delburn Bay the moment she'd discovered Zeke was in Westlake.

Waiting for the right moment had been a mistake, because there was never going to be the perfect opportunity for giving a person that kind of news. And in delaying, she'd only made things ten times worse. A hundred times.

'I have a son?'

His shocked words were barely audible and still the torment in his tone lacerated her. She couldn't even answer. Not that he needed her to. Anyone who saw father and son together would instantly see the resemblance. There was no denying the relationship.

Not that she wanted to.

Hadn't she wanted to tell Zeke about his son five years ago, the moment she'd first discovered she was pregnant?

And she would have, if not for that night.

'Jesus, Tia. I have a son.' He started forward. Determination and anger etched onto his face.

She didn't know how she found the strength but suddenly she was blocking his way, her hand pushing back against his shoulders.

'Not here. Not like this. You can't meet him when you're like…this.'

He turned an incredulous black gaze on her. Tia swallowed hard.

'Zeke, I'm sorry. Sorrier than you can ever know. But please. Don't go in there like this. Don't do that to Seth.'

Zeke didn't answer. His eyes slid back to the closed door, to the happy, high-pitched voice inside, assuring her that her son was oblivious to what was going on out in the hallway. The silence spiralled around her, coiling and menacing. It felt like an eternity before anyone spoke again.

'Seth,' Zeke echoed quietly at last. As though he was rolling it around his head. Letting it sink in. Letting it take root.

'Seth,' she repeated quietly. 'And you will meet him. I promise. But...not like this.'

He turned to look at her again. As though he were seeing her for the first time. And it wasn't a good experience. A shiver rippled over her body.

'I have a child? I'm a father? And you kept him from me all this time?'

'I... I can explain.' It sounded so hollow. So inadequate. 'If you give me a chance.'

For another painstakingly long moment, neither of them moved or spoke. And then, abruptly, Zeke stumbled backwards, out of the front door and onto the drive. As if he didn't know where he was going, but was afraid that if he didn't leave now, he might barge her out of the way and walk into that room to see his son.

'Now, Tia. You will explain it to me *now*.'

Without thinking twice Tia released the door handle, snatched up her car keys and followed him out of the door.

She had one chance to get this right. And so help her if she made a mess of it.

CHAPTER FOUR

HE HAD A CHILD.

A son.

Zeke had repeated it a hundred times. A thousand. Scarcely knowing what to make of this incredible revelation. Trying to understand what this...*thing* was that spiralled deep within him, as though it were slowly boring its way out of some pitch-black, fathomless pit he had long pretended didn't still reside inside him.

Yet he suspected he knew exactly what the thing was. It was a flicker of light, even just a spark, but potentially powerful enough to cast a glorious light over his life. Joy. And pride.

He had a *child.*

He, who had long since resigned himself to the fact that he would never be a father. What was the point? When five years ago he'd pushed away the only woman with whom he could ever have imagined himself being?

He had believed he was doing the right thing, the honourable thing. Sparing her from the burden of being with a man so much less than the one she'd married. He'd been a soldier, strong and fit and *whole*. After the accident, he had barely been able to stand looking at himself in the mirror; he certainly hadn't been able to bear seeing her look at him with that expression of... sympathy. As though he was *less than*.

Pushing her away, sparing her from having to take responsibility for him, had been the one thing he could do back then to prove he was still strong. Still fiercely independent. But even so, realising he had succeeded, that his Tia had walked out of his life for good, had hurt beyond anything he could have believed.

Until now.

Had he really pushed her away? Or had she been only too relieved for the excuse to get him out of her life? To ensure his son never knew that he had a failed soldier as a father? The suspicion eroded in like the leaking battery acid on the engine of his very first motorbike.

Had she been pretending all those times she'd visited in the first few months after the accident? Or had she secretly been looking for a way out with the son she'd never told him about?

Because there was no doubt that Seth *was* his son.

And she'd been a couple of months into her

medical hearts-and-minds tour of duty when his black ops mission had gone wrong. Which meant the boy had to be around four and a half. Tia would have known she was pregnant. She had to have known.

Surely?

He didn't even need to look across at her to know she was sitting, ramrod straight, in the passenger seat of her car. So typically Tia, at her most defensive. He had no idea what was going on inside her head but he was too angry to ask. A blistering, sizzling fury that tore through him and made it impossible to even speak.

And so here he was, driving her to his house in Westlake because he'd left her with no alternative. Not after he'd seen Seth. He had barked orders at her, rapid and harsh, telling her that he had to be back in Westlake for his duty at the lifeboat station but that he wasn't about to walk away without having a conversation about what he'd just discovered.

When he'd ordered her to come with him—hitting low with the accusation that she owed him that much—he'd nevertheless been surprised when Tia had appeared to capitulate without a word of argument, handing him her car keys before ducking momentarily back inside to ask her father to look after her son—*his own son*—for the evening.

He'd asked her what the keys were for and she'd simply jerked her head towards his bike.

'Well, I can hardly ride on the back of that with you,' she'd muttered awkwardly.

'Because?' he'd demanded irritably, knowing it was irrational to take it as a personal criticism, but unable to do anything else.

And she'd levelled a calm gaze at him, her voice quiet but firm.

'Because we're not kids any more, Zeke. That bike represents my years as a rebel, and a thrill-seeker. Now I'm… I have other responsibilities.'

But it was the words she didn't say that had scraped at him the hardest. That, and the fact that the idea of her body pressed so tightly to his for an hour and a half had been simply unimaginable. Although perhaps it would have given him enough distractions to keep his mind off the all too frequent nightmares that he still endured. The screams, the smell, the sights.

How could he have gone from what had happened between them in her office less than half an hour earlier, from such intense desire then, to such burning anger now? And yet, a part of him couldn't seem to regret how intimate they'd been in that lifeboat station.

So what did that say about him?

Yet for the last ninety minutes, they had sat in a tense, unhappy, charged silence. The same images and questions spinning around in his head, more and more insistent as each minute ticked by. His only comfort was that the closer they came to Westlake—to where she had once lived—the more pent-up she was obviously becoming.

Good. He gripped the steering wheel a little tighter. He wanted her uneasy, off-balance. He suspected it was the only way he was going to get answers to questions she might otherwise deflect all too easily.

But was he imagining it to think that she might possibly have returned to Delburn Bay because she'd felt she owed it to him to tell him about his son?

No.

Tia had had years to find him. To tell him. But she hadn't, so he couldn't afford to let sentiment creep in, or to go soft on her. She had betrayed him. Kept him out of his own child's life for years.

Except that you pushed her away.

Zeke struggled to silence the traitorous voice.

And you wouldn't have been much of a role model for the first few years, would you?

And so he merely kept driving until eventually he was nearing Westlake. First passing the terraced row of tiny fishermen cottages where he had endured years of squalor with the cruel, vindictive, bad-tempered hulk of a man who had spent as much time working hard to avoid getting a job as he had actually going out to do whatever menial job he'd been forced to take.

Then down to the promenade with the larger, more impressive detached houses, which boasted glorious sea views, where Tia had lived with her own kind and protective doctor father. Finally, to the lifeboat station where he was due on call in a matter of hours, and where they had first met when he'd been seventeen and she'd been fifteen. He might have held himself back from going anywhere near her that first year, but she had nonetheless burned too wonderfully brightly for anyone to pretend they didn't notice her.

Becoming a volunteer lifeguard had been Zeke's saving grace as a kid. A stop-gap until he turned eighteen and could join the military, since his old man wouldn't agree to sign papers allowing his kid to join up any earlier. After all, the more Zeke had earned, the less his so-called father had decided *he* had to work.

Even now Zeke could remember the urgency, the desperation, he'd felt, waiting to turn eighteen and swearing to himself that he would never, *ever* return to this part of the country, let alone Westlake.

And then he'd met Tia. Sweet and innocent, but with the kind of steely core and heart of courage that men years older than her hadn't possessed. Especially when it came to being out on a rough sea. The attraction had been instantaneous but he had refused to allow himself to succumb. His respect for the crew—and for Tia's father—had been too great.

When his eighteenth birthday had come, he'd joined up just as he'd always planned. But it was the lure of Tia that had had him returning eighteen months later during a month of leave, a trade in hand and well on his way to his first military promotion.

By the time he'd left they had eloped, marrying in secret, before Tia had embarked on her first year of university, following her father's footsteps in studying for a medical degree.

Now Zeke was deliberately driving her past their very history and it was all too easy to map out. Designed to unsettle her before they even got to his home. The problem was that it was also unsettling him, too.

'Why are we going this way?' she snapped out, as though she couldn't bear it any longer. 'Is this some kind of trip down memory lane intended to make me feel guiltier than I already do?'

'Do you?' he challenged, wishing that a part of him didn't revel in the fact that his Tia was still as astute as ever. 'Feel guilty?'

'What kind of a question is that, Zeke? Of course I do. I never wanted you to find out like this. And I certainly never intended...what happened between us in the lifeboat station this afternoon.'

Any thawing he'd begun feeling towards her disappeared in an instant.

So she didn't regret hiding the truth about his son from him all these years. Just the fact that he'd found out. And that he and Tia had been intimate again.

When the hell was he ever going to learn to stay away from this woman?

'But instead of raking up the past, don't you think we should be looking to the future? Working out where we go from here?'

He battled to harden his heart against her.

'You've had over four years with *our* son,' he ground out bitterly. 'Forgive me if I need a few more minutes to adjust to this revelation.'

'Right,' she murmured, lapsing back into silence.

Along the promenade the grey seas churned

and frothed, every now and then smashing against the sea wall and showering their vehicle with a loud, heavy salt shower.

He might have known she wouldn't be able to stay quiet for long.

'It's just that the only thing at this end of the parade is the old lighthouse and…that old piece of waste ground.'

The old waste ground set up from a section of quiet, rocky beach, where the two of them had often gone to be alone when they had finally got together. Where they'd often imagined buying and building a dream home of their own. *When we grow up.*

Well, they'd grown up now. It was just a shame they had never grown up when they'd still been together.

Zeke didn't answer. He just kept going, waiting for the moment when she would be able to see it for herself. The extent of the new life he had managed to build for himself these past few years. His unexpected success—as hollow as it had felt at times, without her to share it with.

The anticipation clung to him like a sodden T-shirt.

And then, beside him, he could sense her sit forward, taking note.

'What the heck is that?' she whispered at length.

The indignation in her tone was only half suppressed. He couldn't help but smile, despite everything.

'You don't like it?'

'It's...' She scowled as though the right adjective wouldn't come. Finally she was forced to concede the truth. 'It's stunning. Gallingly so, really. But still, someone really built here?'

'Someone did,' he agreed.

The sheets of curved, tinted glass that made up the entire frontage of the house mirrored the foaming seas and rolling grey clouds flawlessly. The renovated lighthouse just behind.

'Someone who has a *lot* of money, by the looks of it.' Tia sniffed.

Was it fanciful to imagine he knew exactly what was running through her head right at this moment?

'You begrudge them living here?'

She paused.

'I don't begrudge them, exactly. It's just that... a location this special deserved to have gone to someone who would really love it and cherish it, not just someone with enough money to have bought off our historically entrenched council.'

'Someone like you and I, you mean?' he challenged. 'Building that little beach shack home we always talked about building when we were kids?'

She didn't answer, she merely pressed her lips into a thin line, as Zeke schooled himself. Restraining himself from reacting.

So what if she remembered the dreams they'd once had back in the beginning? Less than a couple of hours ago that might have meant something to him. But not now. Not after discovering he had a son who she had kept from him all this time.

Instantly Zeke shut the earlier moment of weakness out and steeled himself again.

Finding out about Seth had changed everything.

He might have spent the past five years rebuilding his life and making himself into a man worthy of Tia again—making it up to her for shutting her out immediately after the accident. Maybe even winning her back.

But that had been before.

Now he had lost out on the first four years of his son's life. Zeke didn't know how to begin to quell the thunder that rolled through him. He didn't know what his next move would be. He didn't even know how to articulate a single one of the questions powering around his head right now.

He only knew that he had no intention of missing a single week more of Seth's life.

He didn't choose to answer. Instead he smoothed his mouth flat and turned onto the private road and began the slight ascent to the house.

'Zeke.' Tia's voice broke into his thoughts as he turned her car up onto the track to his home. 'We can't just wander up here.'

'Pretty sure we can,' he replied grimly.

'I don't think it's just the old road to the lighthouse any more.' She sounded panicked. 'It looks like it's the driveway now.'

'It is. My driveway.'

There was a beat.

Then another.

'I'm sorry, say again?'

He deliberately delayed a moment before complying.

'I live here. This is my home now.'

'You own it?'

'I bought the land and had it built.' He shrugged, deliberately sidestepping her real question. 'So yes, I own it.'

Her confusion was evident, but still he didn't clarify.

Let her wonder.

Let her consider how he had got himself from

the mess of a man who couldn't even walk in that rehab centre, to the multimillionaire he was now.

It might give him a moment to begin to get a handle on this racing, flip-flopping tangle of emotions.

Hadn't Tia once called him more of a carefully crafted, honed, precious weapon than a man? A lifetime ago when he'd been about to go on a mission and she'd still been at uni, before she'd joined the army medical corps.

She'd meant it as a good-humoured jibe but it had given him some kind of perverse comfort, and he'd held onto that image for years. Right up until the bomb blast had rendered him broken. Useless. Unsalvageable.

Even now, with all this to show for himself, he was constantly clawed at by vicious nightmares. Regrets. Self-recriminations.

Her heart was hammering so brutally inside her chest that Tia was surprised he couldn't hear it. The place looked like a millionaire's fantasy house by the sea.

If Zeke had intended to unsettle her, he had certainly succeeded. With a shaky arm, she reached out and opened the car door. Getting out and standing up was going to take even more effort.

Toying with her. Leaving her off-balance.

Biting her lip, she followed him across the gravel to the sleek metal and glass door. The place didn't even have a normal lock or key like her house. Instead, he had to have some kind of key fob or pin, because the door opened automatically as he approached.

Not just moneyed, then. But serious money.

Her stomach twisted tightly. With money came contacts, and power. What if he decided to use those resources to get custody of Seth? To provide for him in a way that she couldn't?

Hadn't some former work colleague, Jane, from a few years ago lost joint custody of her two children to her ex-husband? He'd successfully argued something about Jane's career as an A & E doctor meaning long, unpredictable hours whilst he himself had just been promoted in his dependable nine-to-five city job. Plus he'd had a new partner who had cared for a child of her own around the same age.

Tia's mind raced, leaving a plume of fear in its wake.

'Do you live here alone?'

The question was out before she could bite it back, not helped by the way Zeke cast her a look over his shoulder but didn't immediately answer.

On autopilot she followed him as he stepped

through a hallway to the lightest, most expansive living room she had ever been in, sleek windows curving from one wall to the other, and from floor to ceiling. Then he spoke.

'There's no one else here, Tia. There never has been. No one who mattered enough to move them in, anyway.'

And she told herself that her heart didn't leap a little. Instead, she forced her legs to carry her across the room to stand in front of those stunning windows and take in the might of Mother Nature at her most volatile.

'There are going to be a lot of shouts in that weather.'

'It has been a force nine gale several miles out there for the past twenty-four hours. The last few teams have been bested.'

She shouldn't say anything. She couldn't give herself away. Tia opened her mouth.

'Be safe out there,' she whispered. 'Don't do anything...typically heroic, Zeke.'

The silence whooshed in on them, like an invisible flood, filling the space and sending them both reeling.

It could have been minutes before they spoke again. It felt like an age.

'You make it sound like you actually care,' he ground out.

'I always cared,' Tia muttered before she could stop herself. 'You were the one who pushed me away, Zeke.'

'Oh, trust me, Tia, it didn't take much pushing.'

Whether it was the coldness of his tone, the injustice of what he was saying, or the fear jostling around inside over her precious son, Tia couldn't be sure, but her temper flared suddenly.

'Oh, no. That's totally unfair. You were the one who said that if I amputated then I would be killing the only life you had ever known as a soldier. You were the one who, for six weeks, told me over and over that you couldn't forgive me. And you were the one who, in that rehab centre, told me that you couldn't bear to look at me and would never, *never*, forgive me.'

'I did it to protect you,' he roared before falling into abrupt silence.

Spinning brusquely, he strode to the couch. She got the sense it was as much to put space between them as anything else, and she was grateful for it. She could barely breathe, let alone think.

The moments ticked by. The silence turning black.

'I did it to release you from the burden of having to be responsible for a cripple. All I'd ever wanted from being a kid was to be a soldier. A marine. I couldn't even get myself out of bed without help.'

'You didn't do it to release me from any burden.' Her heart ached to comfort him, but this was Zeke and she knew him too well. Comforting wouldn't help. She needed to stay strong and meet his accusations head-on. 'You did it because your pride wouldn't let you accept help from me. You didn't trust me enough to let me be there for you. *That's* why you pushed me away, Zeke. No more, no less.'

'You were my wife,' he spat out. 'Who else would I trust?'

Tia was determined to stand fast.

'Which makes it all the more hurtful that you couldn't turn to me, but no less true. If *I* had been the one injured, you would have insisted on never leaving my side. But because it was you, you couldn't bear to have me around. You even told the nursing staff they had to keep me away.'

'You didn't need to see me at that time.'

'Why, Zeke? Because you felt vulnerable and at your lowest? We were married—we should have been a team. We could have been the strongest team. Instead, you never learned to let me in.'

'Of course I let you in. We were married for

ten years, for pity's sake. You knew things about me that no one else has ever known.'

'Such as?'

He glowered, clearly hating every second of this line of argument.

'You knew about where I grew up. My old man.'

'Facts, Zeke.' She blew out a deep breath. 'I knew where you lived because Westlake is a small town and everyone knows everyone. I knew that your dad was a violent, abusive drunk, who took his anger out on you after your mum left, again because everyone knows everyone else's business. But I never knew anything because *you* told me. I never knew how you felt inside, because you never told me.'

She wasn't prepared for the profound sadness that settled inside her, like old dust disturbed from a furniture cover suddenly lifted in a long-abandoned house.

'It was irrelevant,' he gritted out.

'It wasn't.' Tia shook her head. 'That kind of thing makes us who we are. And you never gave me a chance to know that part of you. In truth, Zeke, I don't think we really know each other. We barely ever did.'

'We've known each other for eighteen years,' he snorted.

'You didn't come near me at the beginning because I was fifteen and you decided I was too young,' she pointed out. 'Even though, I hasten to point out, that you were only seventeen back then.'

'Well, we've still been married for the past fifteen years.'

'You can't count the last five of those fifteen years,' Tia argued. 'We've basically spent them apart. The point is that we've never truly understood each other. You never let me in to understand what you thought, or felt, or what made you tick.'

'You already knew all of that. You knew that I was desperate to get out of Westlake. You knew why I joined the army and then the Royal Marines. You knew that my military career was all I had.'

'It wasn't all you had, though,' Tia burst out. 'That's what I'm trying to say but you keep refusing to hear me. You had *me*. You just didn't want me enough.'

She twisted around so he couldn't see the shameful tears threatening to spill over. Still, his harsh reply was like a dagger to her back.

'That's bull.'

It took her a few moments to steady herself. Another few to turn around and face him.

'We were young, and stupid,' she offered shakily. It sounded feeble but it was simpler than the whole story, and it had the benefit of at least being true. 'In real terms we barely even knew each other. I mean, what were we thinking, running off to get married like that? I was only just eighteen, you weren't even twenty.'

'We thought we were in love.'

And there was the truth, in those little words. *Thought we were.* Not simply *were.* Even though she knew he was right, it still hurt.

'We were selfish. And cruel.'

'You mean I was,' he corrected bitterly. 'Because my old man didn't give a damn about anything I did, and I took you even though I knew that you *did* have a father who cared.'

'I mean *we* were. I certainly don't remember you strong-arming me into anything. In fact, I seem to recall it was my idea. I thought it was romantic and daring.'

His jaw clenched in a way that was achingly familiar, and Tia would have given anything to know what he was thinking in that instant.

'Still,' he ground out eventually. 'We made sure you went to uni. I went back to my training. We weren't completely irresponsible.'

'Do you realise that in those ten years of our marriage, when we weren't separated, we saw each other less than fifteen months? Out of one hundred and twenty months?'

'You're rewriting history.' His eyes glittered coldly from all the way across the room. 'We were living our lives, but we were still together.'

'I don't think it's me who's rewriting things.' She shook her head, warning herself to stay strong. To tell him even half the things she'd imagined telling him these past years. 'I once calculated it.'

'Calculated what?'

She breathed deeply, and in that moment she didn't care if he realised how low she must have been at one time, to work it out.

'I calculated that we, in fact, saw each other less than four hundred and fifty days out of over three thousand, six hundred and fifty.'

He blinked, as though taking it in for a moment. His expression darkening.

'I don't recall you complaining much at the time.'

'No, because it was like a protracted honeymoon every time we saw each other, Zeke. Thrilling and wonderful, filled with passion.'

'And *thrilling* was a problem?'

'Yes!' She threw her arms into the air, as though that could somehow articulate her point better than her words could. 'Because there was nothing remotely realistic about it. We weren't like normal couples who live together and get to know each other's quirks and foibles. Who argue over putting the washing out, or whose turn it is to cook, or whether the toilet seat should be up or down.'

'Seriously?'

'You can scoff—' she shook her head at him '—but you know I'm right. We didn't really know each other at all. We were in love with the idealistic image of the kids who had once fallen for each other. We certainly had no real knowledge of the people we were growing into. Of how our careers, our experiences, were moulding us. You can't really tell me you don't see that.'

She peered at him incredulously, those blue eyes holding hers with such authority. But then it hit her, the realisation that he knew exactly what she was saying. That he agreed.

They didn't know each other at all.

It was one thing to know the truth on an intellectual level. It was quite another to see it reflected so clearly in Zeke's gaze.

She faltered, stepping backwards as though she'd been dealt a physical blow. The silence closed in again, and this time a bleakness came with it. She felt as though she were a thin plastic bag caught in a squall, blown this way and that.

'None of which explains why you didn't tell me that you were pregnant,' he said suddenly, breaking through the water that was filling her mind and causing her to resurface. 'Why you've kept my son from me for four years.'

'Zeke.'

'It's funny how the problems of our *protracted honeymoon*, as you called it, only imposed themselves when you realised that my career as a soldier—the thing which had attracted you to me all those years before—was over.'

That wasn't how it had happened but her frustration, and her fears, overtook her.

'My God, Zeke. I was a teenage girl. Show me a teenage girl who isn't swept up by the idea of a strong, good-looking lad intent on becoming some kind of heroic soldier and saving lives? And your monstrous father was what drove you on to be better, and better. It was your way to change who you were and make a difference in the world.'

'And you loved that,' he sneered.

'As a kid...' she heard the desperation in her voice as it rang out '...not as an adult. By the time I was a trauma doctor with several tours under my belt, I knew the reality wasn't anywhere near so poetic.'

'So what *is* the reality, Tia?'

'That nothing would ever be enough for you. You were a maverick, Zeke. Your entire squad was. That was why you got the kind of missions that no one else could ever handle. I may not have known what they were, but I heard the whispers. I knew the rumours.'

'Yet you stayed with me,' he pointed out. 'Because you wanted to be with me. I wasn't just an average bloke you could have met in your student union, I was a marine, and then SBS. I was living life at maximum velocity and you loved that.'

'I was terrified of that,' Tia said quietly. Firmly. 'But I loved *you*. So I accepted that was who you were. Someone who had to keep pushing himself, risking his life, because that was how you had come to define yourself. You guys thought you were invincible, and sometimes you even managed to convince me that you were, too. But then reality would set in, and fear. So, *no*, Zeke, I didn't love it. That last year in particular I watched you walk out the door and expected never to see you again.'

'Then you must have been thanking your lucky stars that I released you from the responsibility of being my wife when I got injured.'

His voice was full of such bitterness and loathing that it clawed inside Tia's chest. She didn't realise she'd sunk onto the rug until she felt the soft material gripped in her hands.

'You really want to know what I thought when you got injured?' she whispered hoarsely, barely recognising her own voice. Every fibre of her being screaming at her to stop talking.

'Why not?' He laughed. A hollow, empty sound. 'It can't be any worse than anything I imagined.'

She swallowed. Sucked in a deep breath. Swallowed again.

'A part of me was relieved,' she managed eventually. So quietly that she wasn't initially sure he'd heard her. But the tense silence in the room told her otherwise. 'A part of me knew that this was the end of your military career—I knew you'd never stay in just to fly a desk—and I was so thankful that I wouldn't have to be scared for you any more.'

'You were glad I was injured,' he echoed. Dark, sharp, lethal.

'No,' she cried, then shrugged helplessly. 'Not exactly. But at least you weren't dead. At least you were still...with me. I thought...maybe...at last...we could finally give our marriage a proper try. But instead, you hated me, you made that abundantly clear. I was the one who had taken your leg and you couldn't forgive me for it.'

He wanted to argue, that much was obvious. He opened his mouth to. But suddenly he couldn't.

It was little comfort.

She had been right. He'd hated her. Not as much as he'd no doubt hated himself, of course.

'You still kept Seth from me,' he choked out at last, but at least he was directing his pain and rage towards her, rather than inward as he might have done during their marriage. Or at least, proper marriage.

He might be mad at her, but he wasn't shutting her out. Surely that had to be a start?

'You had to have known you were pregnant. You would have had every opportunity to tell me. You didn't. You deliberately concealed it. I might have pushed you away, but you were still the one who left. Taking my unborn baby with you.'

'It wasn't like that. I left for both our sakes, Zeke,' she repeated, her voice softer now that she could see he wasn't going to argue with her. 'And for Seth's sake. But please believe me, I never intended to stay away this long.'

He didn't answer, but the expression on his face warned her that he didn't believe her.

'I promise you that I always imagined I'd find you and tell you.'

'When?' Zeke cut in. 'When our son turned eighteen? Got married? Had a family of his own?'

The challenge was clear, but if she hadn't known better, she might have thought she'd heard the briefest of hesitations. As if he might have been on the edge of believing her. As if he had just softened, ever so fractionally, before her eyes.

Not so much that a stranger might notice it, of course. This was Zeke, after all. But she noticed. And it caught her off guard.

But then he shut down on her again, and she knew she must have imagined it.

'You know what, Tia? Forget I asked. I think there have been enough revelations for one night, don't you?'

'I…' She faltered.

'I need time to think. Feel free to leave.'

He stood up, and Tia found herself scrambling to her feet in echo.

'We *will* discuss this further.' Whether he was issuing a threat or a promise, she couldn't be sure. 'I'll come to Delburn Bay when I have a solution.'

Why was he being so cold? What had changed? A chill crept over her skin.

'A solution?'

'Don't disappear,' he continued as if she hadn't even spoken. 'And if you do find your own place, make sure your father knows to tell me *exactly* where that is. I don't intend to have to come searching for you. Or my son.'

He had her halfway out of the door and into her car before she could protest. The darkness of night and whipping wind catching her unawares.

How long had they been in his house? The storm that had been raging way out at sea was clearly beginning to move closer.

'Your motorbike...?' she yelled above the roar.

'I'll collect it another time. I have a car for the meantime.' She followed the jerk of his head towards a sleek double garage more than heard his words. But then he was slamming her door and walking away. Barely stopping to call over his shoulder. 'Goodbye, Tia.'

Mutely, she obeyed, sliding her car fob into the central console and pressing the ignition button and moving inexorably off the drive. She couldn't fight him. She didn't even understand what she was fighting.

Tia was already out of Westlake and on the route home when her mobile rang.

Was it Zeke? Calling to tell her he'd changed his mind?

Dammit, why hadn't she connected to Bluetooth?

Pulling over into a layby, Tia fumbled through her bag, the phone seeming to slip elusively away from her each time. She certainly wasn't prepared for her father to be calling, asking her if she was okay.

'I'm fine. I'm on my way home, why?'

'That's good,' his reassuring voice crackled over the connection. 'As long as you're safe.'

'What is it?' she asked, unable to shake the sense of disquiet.

'It's nothing. I'll see you when you get back here. Drive safely, and if the weather gets too bad, stop at a motel for the night.'

'What's going on, Dad?' It took all her effort to keep her voice calm. 'Please. Tell me.'

And then she listened as her father reluctantly told her that there had been a major incident at sea and that both Westlake and Delburn Bay lifeboat stations had been called on to attend. They would assist with a search and rescue helicopter already flying out to the scene.

Tia didn't think twice. She confirmed that her father was happy to look after Seth for the night, and then she terminated the call, turning her car around and heading back into Westlake.

If there was a shout now, then Zeke was heading out to it. And after the conversation they'd just had—the emotional state his head must surely be in—she couldn't just leave it at that.

She had to be there. She had to know he was safe.

Whatever that said about the way things were between them, now wasn't the time to worry about it.

CHAPTER FIVE

TIA CLUTCHED THE cool resin countertop of the lifeboat station's compact kitchen and waited for Albert—a volunteer who had been at the station from even before she herself had started there aged a mere fifteen—to terminate the radio call and update them. The last few hours had been unbearable, without a single reprieve, and the atmosphere amongst the other volunteers left behind, concerned for their colleagues and feeling helpless, was sombre, at best.

Her only consolation was the fact that Albert had been so absorbed with the shout that he hadn't had a chance to do more than look shocked at her arrival, then hug her tightly, before focussing in on the emergency.

He certainly hadn't had time to ask her any questions, or, worse, reminisce about the good old days when her mother had been a coxswain and her father the medical officer.

As the old man plodded heavily into the room

her heart hammered in her chest, and she fought to try to calm herself.

Even as she had arrived at the station it had been scant relief to hear that the initial report had said that a cargo ship had been slightly listing as a result of some of the hundreds of containers on deck that had shifted in the violent storms. The treacherous conditions at sea had meant that it would most likely take hours before the Delburn and Westlake lifeboats—who had been asked to attend in support of the rescue helicopter taking the lead for the incident—reached the scene.

Now, a few hours later, they were still waiting for news. A temporary loss of radio communications had only heightened the tension all round. Albert cleared his throat, his steadfast, calm voice belied only by the strained lines around his eyes.

'It seems the situation has degenerated. There's about a five-metre swell out there, which has caused the cargo to slide further and made the ship list to such an extent that the portside rails had become submerged. They've lost power and at least two of their crew are already injured.'

'Our guys won't reach them in time,' someone muttered, concerned.

'Zeke has increased his speed to twenty knots

to try to ensure that they do.' Albert's frown deepened.

As the murmurs rippled around the room, Tia's grip tightened. As did the fist around her heart. But she couldn't speak. Couldn't even utter a sound.

'They'll never make it.'

'Those seas will be mountainous; the lifeboat will be tossed around like it's a kid's bath toy.'

'They'll be airborne more than they're in the damned water. They're more likely to injure themselves just getting there than anything else.'

Silence reigned for a moment.

'It's typical Zeke, though, ain't it?'

'Well, if anyone can do it, he can.'

'Yeah. If you want someone coming in for you, it'd be him. And his crew.'

She wanted to scream, and shout, and tell them *what did that matter if he got himself killed in the process?* How did she tell her son? How did she even begin to get him to understand? Especially when she barely understood it herself.

But she didn't say a word. She couldn't. And still, the fears encircled her.

It was pitch black out there; even with the lifeboat's searchlights the lads wouldn't be able to see when the waves were coming at them. Ready to hit them. She could only imagine them holding on tightly as they felt their Atlantic class boat climbing each swell, bracing for the moment they plummeted down the other side, smashing back into the unforgiving sea.

That was if they weren't tossed right out of the water altogether. Spun over. Capsized.

A wave of nausea built inside her.

Most of her knew that he would never risk the lives of his crew members. *Never.* But there was that tiny, fearful part of her that knew that the night of his accident had changed him fundamentally. He'd lived but two of his buddies had died.

Tia swallowed hard. Zeke would trade his life for either of theirs in an instant because he didn't value his life enough. His monster of a father had made sure that Zeke had never really known how to value himself at all.

And that was the knowledge that scared her most.

The wait for more news seemed interminable. And then it came through, and Tia almost wished it hadn't.

Zeke and his crew had arrived as the rescue helicopter was trying to get into position to winch up the men from the cargo vessel, one by one. But the wind had been relentless, buffeting the helicopter time and again, and the sea rolling with such power that it had almost smashed the container ship into the helicopter several times. There was no way this wasn't going to end in tragedy.

And so the terrible decision had been made to pull the helicopter back, leaving the crew on board, preparing to abandon ship. Their only choice to leap into the raging waters and pray that the lifeboats would be able to pull them out before they drowned or were slammed into their own ship.

The chances of recovering all of them, or even most, were slim, at best.

It shouldn't have come as a shock to Tia, or any of them sitting there in that station, that Zeke had come up with a different plan. A mad, dangerous plan. But a plan that only a coxswain of Zeke's skill could even hope to pull off.

And exactly the kind of stunt she'd been talking about back at his house, when she'd said he defined himself by how much he was risking of himself, in order to save another life.

He was going to manoeuvre his lifeboat into such a position that he could take a run up to the stricken ship—a vessel thousands of tonnes heavier than Zeke's own, and which could easily be lifted by the seas only to smash down on top of the smaller lifeboat—and get close enough for the terrified crew to leap from their deck onto his.

The nausea rushed Tia all over again.

It was sheer insanity.

But it was the other crew's only chance of surviving. No wonder Zeke was determined to try. Always the hero. But never to himself.

Cramps sliced through Tia's hands as she realised they were locked onto the countertop, clinging on as though it was the only thing keeping her upright at this moment.

It probably was.

When she'd told Zeke earlier of how terrified she'd been that each time he'd walked out of the door of their home, it might be the last time she ever saw him—she'd failed to convey *exactly* how paralysing that fear had been.

How each day, each night, when people knocked on the door or called her, she would momentarily freeze, a part of her wanting to run away just in case they were bearing news she wouldn't want to hear.

Being on tours of duty of her own had almost been a relief. They had been challenging and exhausting, occupying her mind and giving her something else to focus on. Something to stop her from worrying about her husband.

In fact, she hadn't had to worry about Zeke's

well-being for five years—although a part of her couldn't pretend that she hadn't thought about him every single day. Every time she'd looked at Seth and seen her son's father.

Now here she was, practically hurtling back in time. Only this was worse, far worse, because now she knew what it felt like to lose him. And however much she told herself she didn't have him to lose any more, the idea of breaking this fragile reconnection they'd just made was almost unpalatable.

Which only confirmed one thing. As soon as Zeke got back safely tonight—and he had to, she couldn't accept any other option—she was going to have to find the courage to answer his questions. To try to explain about Seth.

She wouldn't hide behind the argument that he wasn't going to believe her because *so what* if he didn't? She could hold her head up high and say she had tried. The way she'd always imagined doing.

The way she would have done if her weakness back at the lifeboat station hadn't allowed that… intimacy to occur between them. The way she would have done if he hadn't then followed her home and seen Seth before she'd had a chance to explain.

The radio crackled, making her jump, and everything in her clenched painfully.

How immeasurably cruel would it be that the moment Seth and Zeke had finally found each other, Zeke was taken away from his son again?

And what about you?

Tia hastily crushed the whispering voice, but it was too late. The words, the implications, were already coursing through her entire body as if she herself had toppled into those inky-black ice-cold waters that churned outside in the darkness.

'If you end up killing yourself and leaving Seth broken-hearted, Ezekial Jackson,' she muttered so silently that no one else could hear, 'I swear I'll never forgive you.'

And she told herself it meant nothing when her own heart felt as though it were ready to fragment into a million pieces.

One more practice run at it to make sure he fully understood how the two vessels were likely to interact, Zeke thought, and then he would make the first full attempt to rescue the first crewman from the *Queen Aetna*.

The port side of the cargo ship was now fully submerged, an invisible hazard every time he brought the lifeboat too close. But there was nothing else for it. The crewmen would surely perish if he didn't try something.

His men were harnessed up as per his instructions and each were in their positions, whilst the Delburn Bay lifeboat was holding as steady as they could a little further out, their searchlight trying to illuminate as much as possible for his team.

He always felt the responsibility of getting his guys home safely from shouts, back to their families. And it wasn't always a guarantee when you were in a lifeboat crew—the sea could be a fickle, dangerous mistress. But tonight, it felt as if there was another edge to it. A sharper, more brilliant one.

Tonight, *he* had someone he had to make it home for, too.

He had his son.

And Tia.

No, not Tia. Zeke instantly thrust that thought from his head, ignoring the voice that whispered that it was too late to pretend he didn't still care about her.

But certainly Seth.

Thank goodness they were back home where he knew they were all right. Safe.

Icy cold reality raced back in to douse him, to drag him back to where he was. The conditions were atrocious, the noise of the crashing water drowning out anything else. They were all going to need to be flawless in their hand signals, but he trusted his team. Hadn't he trained most, if not all, of them? Not to mention the very real danger that if he overshot his mark, even by a few metres, the cargo ship could crash down onto the lifeboat's bow.

There was no choice. Lives were on the line.

Then, as the storm blasted around them, Zeke made his first real approach only for the sea to open up in a great, unpredictable, menacing yawn. Both vessels rolled.

Then collided.

It took all of Zeke's skill to extract his lifeboat without any serious damage. A lesser coxswain might have bottled it. But that wasn't him.

It never had been.

Maybe Tia saw it as a flaw, his so-called pig-headedness, but he saw it as a fundamental part of his psyche. He would *never* willingly leave a man behind.

Checking his crew were ready, Zeke manoeuvred himself back into position and set about a second approach.

It was three hours, more than seventy approaches and a lifetime of exhaustion before Zeke and his crew—and the Delburn lifeboat—finally turned and headed back for shore.

Twelve of the fourteen crew from the cargo ship were safe on his boat, whilst the other two, who had missed the jump from their sloping deck to his, had been fished out of the water by Delburn's crew.

Not a single man had been left behind, and for that Zeke gave silent thanks. When one of the crewmen had got caught up in a rope as the ship had begun to sink, and all the containers had shifted, both crews had thought he was dead.

If two of his lifeboat crew hadn't taken their lives in their hands and taken out the inflatable lifeboat, he certainly would have drowned.

Even launching the inflatable in those conditions had been hair-raising. But now they were facing a new problem—their main casualty needed emergency medical attention that went way beyond the ability of any of his crew.

'Contact the station, see if they can patch us through to emergency services,' he yelled, his eyes not leaving the churning water, still fighting to cut through the heavy swell and get them home safely. 'Maybe they can advise something we can do to help him.'

He focussed back on his own task of piloting the boat; the last thing he expected was to hear his men say that Tia was at Westlake. Fear and something else he couldn't name bit cruelly into him. Like the tentacles of jellyfish hooking into him, locking him in place, stinging painfully every moment. More than they had any right to do.

Why the hell wasn't she back home? Safe with their son?

And then the pain began to recede as a thought slid, unbidden, into his brain. Had she stayed for him?

If so, was it because she cared? Or because she wanted to finally explain herself?

It shouldn't matter to him either way, and yet something crested inside him, like one of the dark, towering waves out there.

Tia listened as the young first aider relayed how the patient had become caught up in some kind of winch rope during the rescue, which had whipped him around causing him to sustain severe chest and arm injuries.

The lad detailed fractured ribs, bleeding and severe lacerations, which they appeared to be stemming. But it was the tachycardia, breathing issues, hypotension and hypoxia that concerned her most.

'I think you're looking at tension pneumothorax. You're going to need to perform a needle decompression, and you're going to need to act fast.'

'I can't.' The voice held a tinge of panic. 'I don't know how to do that.'

'I understand,' Tia soothed, her mind racing over the equipment he might have available to him on the lifeboat. 'But if you don't then he's going to go into cardiac arrest. So I'm going to talk you through it. You're going to be fine. Okay, so first you'll need something that will reach fully into the thoracic cavity. I would suggest a ten-gauge catheter—it's stiff and it will be long enough.'

She waited whilst he shouted out to his colleagues, the noise on the line only giving her the briefest hint at what it must be like for them on the boat, still slamming through the stormy sea.

'I have it.'

'Good, so now you're going to go back to your patient—he's on the floor, right? Okay, clean the area with whatever sterilising solution you have in your kit and then you need to locate the second intercostal space on the same side as the tension pneumo. So find the clavicle and then move down and that will be the second rib. The soft space below it is your second intercostal. Got it?'

She spoke calmly and slowly, trying to keep

the kid as confident as possible. It wasn't ideal, but they were hours out to sea. Without the procedure, there was no way the injured man was going to make it back to shore alive.

'Now, you need the mid-clavicular line. Okay? Good lad. Right, I'm going to talk you through it, but, just so you're prepared, you're going to go in perpendicular to the chest wall, and make sure you push in deep enough before you pull the catheter off the needle. You'll know you've succeeded if you get a rush of air. And there's often also a degree of spray as well so just make sure you've got protective gear on.'

Tia heard the crackle on the line, and then he told her to proceed, her whole body tensed up on the kid's behalf. Clearly, brightly, she began, only able to imagine what was going on at the other end of the connection.

It felt like an eternity. And she heard his exclamation of relief at the rush of air. Not long after, the signs of hypotension and shock she had diagnosed began to be alleviated.

She sagged back onto her chair. All that was left now was for them to get back to Westlake.

And for Zeke to come back safely.

CHAPTER SIX

'WHAT THE HELL is wrong with you? You could have been seriously injured. Killed.'

'This is why you never left Westlake last night, even though I sent you home?' Zeke kept his voice remarkably calm and even, knowing it would only irk her all the more. 'So you could stay here to berate me?'

But the truth was, he wasn't just keeping calm for Tia. It was the only way to keep at bay the storm of emotions churning inside himself right at that moment. It was why he didn't even bother to turn around as she slammed her car door and stalked up the drive behind him, her heeled boots crunching hastily on the gravel.

He was only slightly galled to realise that, after all that had been said between them less than six hours ago, he still wanted her. He had to fight the urge to stride up to her and haul her body to his. To remind himself that he was alive. That he'd made it back to land safely.

There had been moments out there, during that

shout, when he'd found it impossible to shut out the niggling doubt that—this time—his crew might not make it home. He knew that over the years there had been several times when members of his crew had been concerned. Worried. But he'd never been one of them. He'd believed in fate.

Tonight had been different. Images of Tia, of Seth, had crept into his brain, and with them had come the first tentacles of fear. He'd let himself consider, for the first time in five years, that there was someone worth making it home for.

Two people, in fact.

It was an odd sensation, not exactly unpleasant, but…*strange*.

Why had he never felt this fear back when it had just been him and Tia, off on their own missions? Because there was no doubt that he'd wanted to be with her back then. Yet that worry about not making it home had never existed in the past.

Had Tia been right earlier, when she'd accused him of feeling invincible back then? It was a question that had been circling in the back of his mind ever since she'd said it.

He'd always been so sure of his ability, so proud of his tight-knit squad, that even though he'd known logically that missions could go wrong, in his heart he'd never believed it could happen to *them*.

For the first time, he began to consider how that might have impacted his young wife. But not for long. Tia's voice quickly cut across his musings.

'Well? *Did* you even think about how dangerous what you were doing was?'

'What kind of a question is that? Close the door behind you, Tia, you never know if some raging harridan might follow you in from the street.'

'Very funny. I'm not a raging harridan.'

'I never said you were,' he replied mildly, not even slowing down as he made his way along the corridor, unbuttoning his shirt as he went and hearing her furious, hurried steps tapping down the hallway behind him. 'I merely observed that I wouldn't want one to do so.'

'Of course you did,' she answered snippily, still hot on his heels.

He could pretend it was the adrenalin still racing through him, but he knew that wasn't it. Tia had stayed. For him. And now she was bawling at him because she was concerned.

It should be too little, too late. Yet he was letting her carry on as if he were some starving man and she were throwing him scraps from the bin.

Life was so damned short. It was a fact he already knew well, but tonight had reminded him of it. As if he needed the reminder.

Tia was right: he *had* pushed her away five years ago. He *had* made cruel, devastating, accusations, to drive her from him. Of course, he hadn't known she was pregnant, and he couldn't forgive her for not telling him, but that didn't mean he wasn't determined to be a part of his son's life now that he finally knew Seth existed.

He just hadn't worked out the finer points of *how*, yet. And until he did, all Zeke could do was to keep moving, not stopping long enough for Tia's words—her concern—to get under his skin. To have any real effect.

He just needed to unsettle her long enough to buy himself time to think.

Evidently Tia didn't realise where he was heading until he strode into his en-suite bathroom, dropped his shirt and tee into the laundry basket, and had his hands on his open jeans waistband.

She pulled up sharply as he'd anticipated. Just the way she had less than a day earlier in the lifeboat station. Her eyes lingering a fraction too long, pooling a fraction too dark, before she tore them away and scanned behind her to realise they'd just walked through his bedroom.

'I take it that you intend to join me.' His tone was deceptively conversational. 'I must say it isn't the reaction I'd anticipated, but I guess I'm not complaining.'

For a moment her forehead furrowed in a way that was achingly familiar, then realisation crossed her features and then, oddly, anger.

'Is this seriously a joke to you?'

Her tone was sharp, but her tongue flickering out over her lips betrayed her.

And fascinated him.

Which made it almost more dangerous than being out in that rolling sea. Suddenly, it didn't seem so wise after all. *Damn her for always finding a way to creep under his skin.* Irritation slammed through him.

'Not in the least. So if you don't want to join me, I suggest you get out.'

If he hadn't been ready, hadn't steeled himself against it, it might have got to him when she flinched as she did. It might have felt like a weight on his soul.

Then, wordlessly, she turned and left the room, leaving him to shower in what he told himself was peace.

He half expected her to have left when he

emerged. Told himself it was irritation he felt, not exhilaration, when he saw her still there in his living room. He was glad he'd thought to slip on black jeans to cover the limb. He'd never taken pains to hide it in front of anyone else.

Only Tia could make him feel so irrationally conscious of it. As though he was worried it might make her see him as anything less than fully competent to step up to the role as father to his own son. It was disability he'd spent years proving to the world it didn't have to be. At least tonight had proved him as capable as any other volunteer on that lifeboat. More so.

Though it was galling that he should need to prove anything to her.

'Had your fun?' she asked pointedly, jerking her head up as he approached.

Did he imagine that flicker of weariness in her voice? Perhaps he did. Perhaps not. Either way, he knew he was done with them taking potshots at each other.

'I'm sure we could go on for what's left of this night firing questions at each other, until that hint of light on the horizon out there stretches into fully fledged morning, but I'm not really sure it's getting us anywhere. Are you?'

'I don't know, Zeke—do you think that could

be because you counter all of my questions with one of your own?'

'You don't find that a touch hypocritical?' he pointed out before finally relenting. 'Fine. Yes, I considered the danger, but those men would have been dead without us. Anyone else would have done the same.'

Flames of fury licked at her expression.

'I'm not so sure.'

'Meaning what?'

Lovely as ever, she arched her eyebrows at him.

'Meaning you've always been a risk-taker, Zeke. I think you live for that danger. I think you can't live without it.'

'You're wrong,' he ground out, but something shifted uncomfortably within him. A tiny part of him that suspected she was right.

The silence shrouded them and then, abruptly, the fight went out of her.

'This was a mistake.'

It was the quiet sadness in her tone that really scraped at him.

'What was a mistake?'

'Coming back here. Trying to tell you about Seth.'

It was like a punch to the gut and ray of hope all at once.

'I'm his father. Now I know that he exists I won't let you shut me out of his life ever again. I'll be there for him.'

'You're a liability,' she snapped.

'Say again?' He had never been a violent man—he'd had enough of that growing up with a father like his—but right now he could have punched a hole through his very walls.

'Tonight was a miracle, Zeke. You got those men to safety and kept your own crew safe. But what would have happened if you'd been just a metre out? Just once? Would everyone have made it back alive then? Would you have made it back alive?'

'But we did.'

'Lord knows how.' Her breath hitched in her throat but she forced it out. 'And what of Seth, your son, then?'

'That didn't happen, Tia.' His voice was low, lethal. It was all he could do to keep his cool.

'This time,' she emphasised. 'But what is your plan, Zeke? To build a relationship with Seth? To get close to him? To get me to agree to tell him who you really are so that he can love you as the father he's always dreamed of?'

'You have a real problem with that, don't you? Why?' he roared.

'Why do you think, Zeke? Because what happens to him, then, next time you go off to pull a stunt like tonight? When, that time, it doesn't work out quite so spectacularly?'

'That's the reality of life, Tia,' he managed, but the words jarred unexpectedly, even to his own ears. 'We can't protect people against horrible things, no matter how much we want to.'

Tia seemed to slump, as though relieved and devastated all at once.

'But I can try to protect my son from as much pain as possible. Especially when it's so inevitable. You have a self-destructive streak, Zeke, you always have had. We both know it. If there's a burning building you would have to be the first one to rush in and risk your life even if the fire service were minutes out.'

'Minutes could make a difference,' he countered, not wanting to concede her point.

'I'm not putting our son through that.' She stood fast.

'You think you can *not* tell him about me?'

'I think it's my duty as his mother to protect him. Whatever noble cause you dress it up as, how can I bring you into his life when I know that one day I will have to get him through the inevitable pain of losing you because the only way you can feel alive is by risking your life?'

'You seemed to have no trouble getting through

that so-called pain,' he levelled at her, unable to help himself.

'No trouble?' she cried. 'You told me never to come near you again. That I'd ruined your life and you could never forgive me.'

This was ridiculous; they were going around in circles. But then, maybe that was the point—they had never really learned to talk to one another. They'd never tackled issues or ironed out differences. Maybe Tia was right, they had viewed the whole ten years of their marriage as an extended honeymoon period, never needing to get into the nitty-gritty of relationship bumps in the road because before anything became an issue one or both of them would have been leaving, off on some tour of duty or something.

Except that last time. And then he'd metaphorically drop-kicked her out of his life.

For her own good, Zeke reminded himself fiercely. Yet it didn't drown out the whispering voice that cast doubt. *Or to prevent her from seeing you in any kind of weakened state?*

'I already told you that I said that to protect you. You never once told me that you were carrying our son.'

'You level that at me as an accusation,' Tia cried. 'As though knowing I was pregnant would have changed things. But would it have changed anything, Zeke?'

'Yes.'

'Really? Only, I'm not so sure.'

'Of course it would have,' he bellowed, staring at her incredulously, white-hot anger searing through him. 'It would have changed everything.'

Tia didn't reply, she only watched him. Blinking once. Gently.

A wretched truth began to creep in. Or at least, a suspicion of a truth.

Would it have changed everything? Would it have changed anything?

'Of course it would have,' he repeated.

But this time he was less forceful.

She took a half a step closer to him, though he wasn't even sure she herself was aware of doing so.

'Are you sure?' she pressed softly. 'You told me that you were protecting me. Trying to absolve me of all culpability for amputating in the first place. Trying to free me of the burden that you saw yourself to be. Would you really have changed your mind because of a baby?'

He wanted to repeat that it would. To convince her. But suddenly, he wasn't even sure he was convinced himself.

He'd been a mess in those early months after

he'd got back to the UK hospital. He'd only lost his leg but back then it had felt as though his whole life were over. He'd gone from an exceptionally fit Special Forces soldier, risking his life to protect his country, and those he loved, every day, to not even being able to walk, let alone look after himself; the idea of Tia having to run around nursemaiding him had felt too much to bear. Too shameful. Too humiliating.

How would he have felt knowing they had a baby on the way?

Knowing that when their son cried, he wouldn't be able to get up and go to him; couldn't simply stand and reach over the cot to pick him up; couldn't carry him back to Tia for feeding.

All things normal people took for granted.

Hell, he could barely look after himself those first few months, he couldn't have contemplated being able to take care of a baby. Tia would have been running around after their child, and then running around after him.

He couldn't have borne it.

Darkness rippled within him as a pain stabbed through his arm. It took Zeke a moment to realise he'd been clenching his fist tightly, and his wrist—also damaged in the blast five years ago—was screaming in protest.

Releasing Tia from what he'd feared would be

a lifetime of feeling trapped had been one thing, but the realisation that he had effectively turned his back on his pregnant wife, his future child? That felt like something different entirely.

'Perhaps that's the truth,' he ground out. 'But I can't know for certain, can I? Because you never afforded me that courtesy. You concealed it from me for months whilst I was in that rehab centre. Visiting me every day despite me telling you— shouting at you—to stay away.'

'Not for months.' Tia sucked in a shaky breath. 'Actually, not at all during that time. I didn't know I was pregnant.'

It was pathetic how hope sprang up so instantly within him. He stomped it down savagely. His tone harsher than ever.

'You were on a tour of duty for three months before I got caught in that IED blast. You would have known.'

'But I didn't.'

'You expect me to believe that?'

'You'll believe whatever you want,' she cried in frustration. 'You always do, Zeke, that's the point. But if you're asking me for the truth, it's that I had no idea. Our jobs pushed us, always training, often in danger, and I was never... regular. You know that. I could go six months without having to worry about anything like that.

So I just put it down to the stress of your accident, and the amputation.'

'You visited me in that centre day after day. However many times I told you to stay away, to give me space. You kept coming back.'

Right up until he'd finally found a way to keep her away. The day he'd lied to her and told her that he could never forgive her for what she'd done.

For a long moment they simply stared at each other. Neither of them apparently wanting to talk about that final argument.

'I didn't know.' Her desperation was almost enough to convince him. 'I stayed away because…you were so adamant. Because the nursing staff believed that I was doing more harm than good by visiting. Because I thought if I gave you space, maybe you'd find a way to forgive me for making the only choice I could possibly have made.

'But I swear to you, Zeke, it was only after that I began to suspect I was pregnant.'

'And yet you never came back to me,' he growled.

'How could I? I was afraid that putting additional pressure on you would be damaging. I was warned to let you come to terms with the amputation in your own time.' She flung her arms out helplessly.

'Warned?'

'By the staff at the centre. You were so closed off, it worried everyone. And I was in an impossible situation, Zeke. I wanted to tell you because I hoped it might give you something positive to hold onto, and to work towards. Yet at the same time, I was terrified that you would try to rush your recovery. I was terrified you would push yourself too hard because you felt as though you had to be the one providing for us. For me, and for Seth.'

'That was my job to look after you both. I was his father. I *am* his father.'

The frustration was so thick, so deep, so bitter, he could almost drown in it. And he felt hot, too hot. If he hadn't known better then he might have thought the carefully regulated temperature of his hi-tech home was failing.

'You'd already told me to stay away,' she countered, and he couldn't tell whether she was more furious or sad. 'How could I have loaded that onto you? I figured that I'd give you a bit of space, maybe a couple of weeks, even a month. I thought I had time. But I used to call them. Every day, Zeke. You have to believe that.'

Without warning she moved towards him and placed her hand on his arm.

The effect was electric. Shooting up his arm and through his body in an instant. He could feel her everywhere, and the ache slammed into him with all the force of those metres-high waves on his lifeboat barely a few hours earlier.

'They gave me updates and warned me that you were in a bad place. Survivor's guilt was bandied about for a long while. Hardly a surprise, but it was stopping you from recovering as you should. There was no way you were ready to be told you had a baby on the way. So I knew that staying away from you was the only way you were going to heal. Mentally and physically. Or do you really deny that?'

He hated that she was right.

And he hated the fact that his inability to come to terms with what had happened to him that night had caused Tia to stay away from him. And to keep his son away from him.

Zeke seethed inwardly.

Ultimately, it meant that however much he had congratulated himself on pulling out of that bleak place and setting up a company that he could never have anticipated would take off as it had, he was a failure after all.

Because he'd failed his family.

Stalking the room, he bit back one cruel, damning comeback after another. What was the point in them? The only person who really deserved his condemnation was himself. Tia couldn't hate him any more than he loathed himself right now.

'So I kept calling them each day, until one day I called and they told me you had discharged yourself. They'd thought you would be with me, but you weren't. Of course you weren't,' she choked out, anger and sadness inextricably interlinked.

No, he'd wanted to get as far away from her as possible. Because the temptation to go to her, to be with her, had been too great. He'd feared he might succumb and he'd been determined that the only time he would seek his wife out again would have been when he was strong enough to provide for her again.

He hadn't banked on her leaving her medical career in the army. Effectively disappearing herself. He hadn't for a moment imagined that she'd done so because she had a baby. A son.

His son.

It slammed into him, thrilling and proud, even if somewhat unsettling. And rumbling behind it, unsteadily and weaving a little, a ball of something that felt strangely like joy. He scarcely knew where to start.

'Maybe I *did* need you to stay away from me

in order for me to get myself together,' he conceded at last. Ungraciously. 'But you're lying if you say you did it for me. You did it because it suited you, too. Because you didn't want to be around me. Because you didn't want me as father to our baby.'

Everything inside him was coiled up. Waiting. Desperate. Wanting her response.

It was like a fresh kind of hell when she dropped her eyes from his, unable to deny it.

'I didn't want the gung-ho Zeke. The man who basically jumped at any chance to risk his life. I didn't want my child relegated to having to remember his father as some dead hero. I didn't want him to have to wonder—every single day—if you were going to walk through that front door, the way I had to with my mother.'

Tia's voice cracked, and for a moment Zeke almost floundered. He remembered how lost and alone he'd thought she was the first time he met her. It had never occurred to him that she had carried that weight around her neck all those years—right up to becoming a mother herself; perhaps it should have.

'I'm so sorry...' he began, but she turned on him, practically stumbling over angry words in an effort to cut him off.

'I never wanted him to go through the pain I

went through the night when she hurried out that door to the shout, kissing me and telling me that she'd be there when I woke in the morning. But she…she never was.'

Something kicked at him. Something he didn't care to name.

'I never realised… I'm so sorry, Tia.'

She dashed a furious hand over her eyes.

'I don't need your sympathy, Zeke. I just wanted you to understand.'

'I do understand now,' he started.

'Not understand why I was frightened back then.' She shook her head wildly. 'I mean to understand why—after your heroics last night—I still don't want you in Seth's life.'

He stood, dumbfounded, feeling as if he'd been sucker-punched. It was impossible even to draw a breath.

'I don't want you to walk into my son's life, and fulfil every childish fantasy he ever had, only to leave it again when something happens to you. Because it *will* happen, Zeke. I came back here because I heard you were here, and I thought you'd changed. But you haven't learned to value your life at all, I see that now.'

How was it possible to feel the loss of something he hadn't even known? And yet he felt it. Acutely. Unbearably. As if his son were being ripped from him, despite the fact that they'd never really had a chance to know each other.

'That's where you're wrong,' he ground out, his mouth feeling wholly alien. 'I *am* Seth's father and I *am* going to be in his life.'

'No.' She snapped her head up. 'I can't allow it. I won't.'

'And *I* won't allow you to shut me out of his life any longer. Not only do I intend to spend time getting to know my son, I intend to take him with me when I leave for France in a few days.'

Her laugh was a sharp, hollow sound.

'This time you really *must* be joking. You think I'm going to let you take him out of the country?'

'I know you are.'

She drew her lips into a thin line. Her eyes narrowing. Ready to fight.

'Over my dead body.'

When had that part of her developed? It wasn't a characteristic of Tia's he'd easily recognised. Yet even through his fury he knew it was appealing to a side of him that had never stopped hankering after *what might have been* between them.

She made to move away. To walk out of his house. Out of his life.

He couldn't let that happen.

Dimly, Zeke was aware that he hadn't fully engaged his brain before his mouth was firing away.

'I don't think that's going to be necessary.' He forced his voice to sound even. 'You're welcome to come with us.'

'I'm not going anywhere.' She snorted. 'And there's no way you're taking my son.'

'*Our* son.'

'Fine. But Seth still isn't going with you.'

'Ever heard of Z-Black, Tia?'

She stopped, her brow furrowing, and he had to fight the urge to reach out and smooth it flat. *Ridiculous.* But she was like a narcotic. An addiction he couldn't seem to kick no matter how hard he tried.

'Who hasn't? At least, in the military world.' She lifted her shoulders. 'What does that have to do with anything, though?'

'What do you know about them?' he pressed.

'Why?'

'Answer me, Tia.'

She glared, then sighed.

'Fine. I know they're renowned for prepping civilians for going into war zones, from foreign correspondents to aid agencies, even corporate individuals for restructure. Z-Black is known as one of the best for training them, showing them how to spot for mines, how to look after themselves, how to work with their close protection teams so they don't actually become a liability themselves.'

'You know quite a bit, then.'

'Yeah, they also train up their own close protection teams for both foreign and domestic scenarios. Rumour has it they're into a heck of a lot more than that, but their guys are immensely loyal and no one on the inside has ever confirmed anything. You work for them?'

'Not exactly.' He could have simply told her, but he wanted to see if she would come to it on her own. If a part of her believed in him enough. 'What do you think the Z and the Black stand for?'

'Black is black ops.' She pursed her lips, moments before her eyes widened. 'The Z…is you?'

'Me. And also the other two founding partners. Brothers, William and Frazer Zane.'

He wasn't surprised when she didn't laugh with him. He could well imagine what was going through her head.

'You couldn't.' She paled. 'You wouldn't use Z-Black to take Seth from me.'

'Then don't make me, Tia. Don't take my son from me.'

It was shocking, inexplicable, this…bond… he felt with a boy he'd seen for barely a few moments. He hardly knew what to make of it. He only knew it was potentially the best news he'd ever heard in his life.

'This house…' she managed, sweeping around as if taking it in all over again. 'You and your partners must be millionaires? You're going to use that against me if I fight you.'

'Multimillionaires,' he corrected. The three of them weren't far off billionaire status, but Tia didn't need to know that right now. 'And I don't want to use anything to fight you, Tia. Just don't back me into a corner where I have no other choice. Seth is my son, too.'

She looked as though she wanted to argue. Perhaps wisely, she bit the words back.

'Why France?'

'That's where our training sites are based. More room. I'm going back to oversee a course and I'm taking my son so that we can start to get to know each other. You don't start work officially for a month. Or so you said before.'

'No, but…'

'Coincidentally, Z-Black currently has a need for a medical trainer with experience out in a hostile environment.' Or, at least, it would after he'd made a phone call. 'Which leaves you with two choices, Tia.' He paused, forced himself to smile, as if he found some perverse pleasure in this awful scenario. 'Either you watch me take my son with me. Or you take this role and come with us as a sort of a family.'

'No,' she whispered, her hand fluttering at her chest.

'Then my son and I will go alone. I have a housekeeper who has nine grandchildren she's forever showing me new photos of. She can show me anything I need to know.'

'You're not taking Seth out of the country without me.'

He hated himself for doing it to her, but there was no way he wasn't going to take the opportunity to get to know his son away from the distractions of everyday life. It was too vital not to get right.

'I'm taking the opportunity to get to know my son. I told you, you're welcome to come too— that option still stands. To my mind, Tia, it's a no-brainer. But then that's just my opinion. The choice, as they say, is yours.'

CHAPTER SEVEN

THE CHATEAU WAS bathed in the most stunning sunset as their black, muscular four-by-four powered up the endless, winding tree-lined driveway. It rose out of its setting of verdant sprawling vineyards in stunning yellow stonework which made it seem warm and welcoming—even the single stunning turret wasn't imposing and hostile, like its owner—whilst the pretty shutters only enhanced the romantic feel of the property.

Yet as the car sped over the uneven ground with a light bump, Tia's heart gave a far more violent jerk. She didn't know what unsettled her the most: the fact that she'd allowed Zeke to command her to bring herself and Seth to live with him whilst he got to know his—their—son, the fact that Z-Black was a private chateau in the south of France, or the fact that he had flown them out on a private plane.

Now they were here her sense of unease only intensified.

It was all a world away from the Zeke she

had known, the Zeke she had married, and she couldn't shake the impression that this was his way of showing her exactly that. Proving to her that she didn't know the first thing about him any more.

Maybe it was unintentional. More likely it was a deliberate attempt to unnerve her.

Either way, it was certainly working. She'd been worried enough about the custody angle when she'd seen his home back in Westlake. This was a hundred times worse.

And so she did the only thing she could—she reached for something solid, something which could ground her, something which mattered.

Seth.

'He's still asleep,' she murmured, stroking the soft hair above his brow in the way that always gave her comfort. 'It seems a shame to have to wake him. It has been a tumultuous couple of days.'

Too late, she realised it probably sounded as if she were making a dig at Zeke. She lifted her eyes, opening her mouth to clarify, but the hostile expression that greeted her made her close it again.

'Which is why I've heeded your request not to tell my son who I am,' Zeke ground out before adding darkly, 'Yet.'

Tia swallowed.

'And I appreciate that. I think…it would help for him to get to know you a little before dropping that bombshell on him.'

'The way you dropped it on me, you mean?'

For the second time in as many minutes she opened her mouth only to close it again. Zeke had her boxed in. And he knew it.

They sat in silence for the next few minutes— though it might as well have been years—whilst the vehicle finally pulled up outside the house.

Before she realised it, Zeke had scooped his still-sleeping son up into his arms and was lifting him out of the car and carrying him to the door, with her scurrying to catch up.

Father and son. Leaving her behind. Wasn't this partly what she had feared by coming back into his life? That, or watching him reject Seth as his son. The way he had rejected *her* almost six years ago.

Ironic how she outwardly objected to him ordering her around, demanding that she and Seth join him in France, and yet it was that very commandeering front that made her feel they were wanted. *Required.* She certainly couldn't believe she'd ever considered that Zeke rejecting Seth would be a possibility.

And there it was, the unpredictability that had

always been Ezekial Jackson. The reason she had *let* him reject her back then. Not fighting for him, or their fragile marriage, the way a part of her had so desperately longed to do.

Because she'd known that he'd been dealing with enough just coming to terms with losing his leg. Just trying to find a way to piece his life back together and work out a new path for himself, and for his future.

She'd already explained to him the reasons for her keeping Seth a secret, and they were true. But it hadn't stopped a part of her from always railing against the fact that her son didn't know his father, especially one he could be proud of like Zeke.

The fact that he'd started Z-Black certainly explained how he'd dropped off-grid after leaving the rehab's home. And why the first time she'd heard of him was years later when the newspaper had run those reports about Zeke, the hero coxswain.

Despite herself, Tia felt a soft smile toying with her mouth as she followed Zeke upstairs, still cradling Seth in his arms.

There were so many Zeke-like traits that she recognised. As bizarre as it might seem to a casual onlooker, she knew him well enough to understand why a multimillionaire would be working as a coxswain for a lifeboat charity. The sea ran through his blood, much as it did hers. It was who he was, and it was what he loved.

The Westlake connection still baffled her, though. Why had he come back there, of all places, to be a coxswain? He'd hated the place. Barely able to hang around at the scene of his awful childhood once he'd become old enough to join up.

If she hadn't known better she might have fancifully imagined that he'd come back because of the connection to her. To the way they had first met.

Tia hastily shut the idea down. To believe that was foolhardy. He wouldn't have come back for her. Ever. If there was one thing Zeke had never been, it was sentimental. But then, what had that angry young man, dragged up in a town of people who looked down on him, ever, *ever* had to feel sentimental about?

No, he hadn't come back for her. She couldn't allow herself to think that way. She didn't *want* him to have come back for her. It was too raw, too electrifying. She'd spent her entire youth terrified that every time her mother walked out of the front door that would be the last time they would ever see each other, and then it had happened.

Somehow, Zeke—charismatic, indomitable Zeke—had convinced her that he was bullet-proof. That he would *always* walk back through their front door.

Until he hadn't. And the pain had been intolerable.

And now he was back to playing the hero, only this time behind the helm of a lifeboat rather than behind the trigger of a rifle.

She wouldn't put herself through that again. More to the point, she wouldn't put Seth through that.

And yet here she was, watching Zeke tenderly carry their son. Like the most precious cargo.

'Where does a fish keep its money?' Seth had gleefully asked during the flight—before exhaustion had finally overwhelmed him.

'I don't know.' Zeke had pondered thoughtfully, and then proceeded to offer a myriad solutions, each one more absurd than the last and eliciting howls of laughter from a delighted Seth.

In the end, their son had almost been reluctant to answer, knowing it would be the end of the hilarious and outlandish suggestions from the man who had suddenly, unequivocally, entered his little life.

'In the riverbank,' Seth had announced proudly, his tiny chest positively swelling as Zeke had slapped his palm to his forehead and proclaimed how silly he'd been for not realising and then had wonderfully hammed up how impressed he was.

Now, hurrying behind them both to her temporary bedroom, Tia shook her head. As if that could somehow reorder the jumble of thoughts churning around in there, each vying for pole position.

'These are your rooms,' he announced, kicking open the slightly ajar door with one foot and striding inside. 'I'd have given you the tour but I had a feeling you would want to stay with Seth so he doesn't wake up alone in a strange bed. Your luggage will be brought up imminently.'

'This will be just fine,' she murmured, taking in the room, which was probably about the size of a small Parisian apartment. The sheer grandeur of it making her feel gawkish and out of place.

Another reminder that Zeke was now a multimillionaire, who could probably afford to pay the best lawyers to win custody of Seth—if he so chose. He might not have outwardly threatened to do just that, but it was there, simmering below the surface.

It should twist her in knots. But it didn't.

Why?

Because a part of her truly believed, deep down,

that Zeke would never do that to her or Seth. Was she being naïve?

She hovered as Zeke laid Seth gently on the bed before moving to an ornate blanket box and taking out a colourful throw to cover his son.

'This is Seth's room,' Zeke informed her pointedly, before indicating across to the far wall. 'Your rooms are through that adjoining door. Feel free to freshen up, even take a nap. I imagine it has been a fairly stressful seventy-two hours. Dinner will be in two hours in the large dining room. I'll give you the tour after that.'

'So formal for just the three of us?'

'Actually I thought Seth might prefer to eat a little earlier with some of Mme Leroy's grandchildren, since she babysits them from school every day before her daughter can collect them. Just for tonight whilst we discuss the ground rules whilst you are here.'

'I'm to have ground rules?' She smiled a little too tightly, but Zeke ignored her.

'I always hear them having a lot of fun, and then you can get him into bed before you come down. Besides, some of my senior instructors usually dine over here so that they can brief me on the day's events.'

Of course they did. Because work always came first with Zeke. It was one of the qualities that had drawn her to his young self. But it was also one of the ways he'd kept himself closed off from her—even if she'd never appreciated it at the time.

Zeke was deep in conversation with one of the instructors when Tia made her way down the stairs a couple of hours later, yet he was aware of her presence before he even saw her. Tiny hairs on his body standing to attention, as though the entire aura of the room had changed just by her approaching it.

And then she walked in looking like any single one of his fantasies over the last few years despite the fact that she was in nothing more dressed up than a light grey, soft cashmere jumper over a pair of charcoal trousers and those things he was pretty sure they called ballet pumps on her feet.

Her hair was piled up on her head as though she'd thrown it up there having only just got out of bed. A fact that was belied by the faint mandarin scent of shower gel as she glided gracefully up to him.

How he wished he could dismiss the others now and just have the evening with this arresting creature, as every part of him screamed *mine*.

'Gentlemen, I don't believe you've met Dr Antonia Farringdale before.'

'I most certainly have not had that pleasure.'

Zane. He might have known his old marine buddy wouldn't be able to resist her and as ridiculous, as schoolyard, as it was Zeke couldn't help himself—he took a tiny step forward, so subtle it looked simply as though he were shifting his weight from one foot to the other, but enough that his shoulder was tilted towards the newcomer.

The sense of possessiveness that charged through him caught him off guard. He wondered what a body language expert might make of it. He didn't desire Tia. He couldn't possibly. Not after she'd lied to him. *Denied* him, all these years.

He tried to hold onto the fury, the rage, that had almost overtaken him two nights ago when he'd found out that he had a son. *A son.* And yet he found he couldn't. That initial rage had waned the instant she'd left his house in Westlake that first day. All her words, her admissions, rolling around his head.

He hadn't wanted to understand her excuses, let alone believe them, and yet even then he'd known that he didn't matter.

Only Seth mattered.

And feuding parents would be the last thing the four-year-old boy would need.

Yet if it was only about Seth, and not about Tia, then why was it he still couldn't quite bring himself to relinquish his defensive stance as he introduced her to the room? Starting with his old buddy.

'Tia, allow me to introduce Zane, otherwise known as William Zane. One of the other Zs in Z-Black.'

'William.' Tia smiled and the openness and brilliance of it almost knocked Zeke for six.

How had he forgotten how powerful that smile of hers could be?

He ignored the voice that told him that he hadn't forgotten. Not for a moment.

'Zane, please,' his buddy corrected, beaming back.

Making Zeke uncharacteristically long to punch him in the mouth.

'Zane.' Tia inclined her head. 'You guys have got a great place here.'

'Thanks. We're kinda proud of it.'

'It pays the bills.' Zeke grinned, though it turned into more of an uncomfortable baring of teeth. 'Shall we finish introductions and then eat?'

He'd like to have thought that his companions didn't notice—possibly the others didn't—but Zane and Tia eyed him a fraction too long. A fraction too intently. Then the moment passed, and the evening unfolded relatively easily after that, with the meal passing smoothly and the conversation covering the day's events, as it always did.

But for once, Zeke couldn't concentrate.

He felt completely out of control, watching her eat, straining to hear her own soft conversations. Especially those with Zane, a lothario by his buddy's own admission.

'Would you prefer that we all left so that you and your wife could become a little less *estranged*?' Zane murmured, catching Zeke off guard. 'Perhaps I should warn the guys that you might not make it out into the training village tomorrow.'

'Bull,' Zeke gritted out. 'There's nothing between Tia and me. I'll be there.'

But his tone was too thick and too dark; it revealed far too much.

'Yes, I can tell that by the way you're both taking great pains to look anywhere but at each other.' Zane's eyes gleamed with amusement. 'To talk to every other person at this table but one another. Fascinating.'

'Sod off,' Zeke grumbled.

But it was too late. There was something taking flight within him.

Hope.

Forget all his vows to himself that he wasn't going near Tia again. All he wanted was for his business partner and the instructors to be gone so that he could be alone with her.

'I've been toying with a potential new business venture,' he growled. 'We can discuss it in my study after the meal.'

'That desperate to keep your distance from her, huh?' Zane grinned. 'Man, you must have it bad.'

It took everything Zeke had not to let his eyes slide to Tia.

'You're clutching, mate. We'll have a drink and talk business tactics.'

'Can't.' Zane sloshed down a mouthful of red wine. 'I have a cheeky little rendezvous lined up for later. I've been chasing this one for weeks.'

'Bloody hell, Zane. Not one of the staff? I can't lose another one who can't bear to stay around here and see you with another woman.'

'Once, that's happened once.'

'Twice.' Zeke raised an eyebrow.

'Fine, twice. But I always tell them *no strings*.'

'And they always think they can change you into *marriage and kids*. Thing is, Zane, one day one of them will, and you won't know what's hit you.'

'True.' Zane eyed Tia speculatively. 'But now

I've seen you two together, and heard you talk about your kid non-stop practically all night, I'm beginning to see why *you've* never once been tempted by the fluttering girls who've thrown themselves at you over the past few years.'

'The two are mutually exclusive,' Zeke growled, only for his buddy to snort loudly.

'Yeah, sure. Anyway, I'll leave you to it.'

And then, Zane was boldly making his excuses, citing an early start and swaggering out of the room, leaving Zeke to mull over his buddy's revelations. Lost in his thoughts, he barely registered the evening drawing to a close until he found himself, finally, alone again with Tia.

'I... I should get Seth and head for bed.' She hovered across the room from him.

He ought to encourage her to go.

'If you're happy to leave Seth a little longer, let me give you that tour.'

She eyed him from under lowered lashes, as though she couldn't decide whether she was going to accompany him or not.

'He's still with Mme Leroy. His sleep this afternoon meant he wasn't ready for bed at the usual time,' she murmured at length. 'Perhaps it's a good opportunity to find my way around the place. It is rather expansive.'

Zeke resisted the urge to take her hand and lead her out. Just.

He started with the rooms closest to where they were, forcing himself to impart a few of the interesting facts that Mme Leroy had insisted on telling him, enjoying the way she laughed, encouraged when she couldn't curb her curiosity about the history of the place any longer and started to ask her own questions.

They moved around the building, slowly warming up to each other again. The thaw that had begun over the last couple of days now accelerating. For a moment, here and there, he could swear they both forgot what had brought them here.

How it had brought them here.

Zeke led Tia out onto the terrace and the pool area.

'I didn't bring a swimsuit.' Tia sounded dismayed.

He bit his tongue before he could suggest she didn't need to worry about wearing one. The very idea of it leaving him hard, and aching.

'I can have someone bring you anything you need.'

It wasn't the right thing to say. A reminder of his money, his power. And the fact that she already didn't trust him.

The thaw slid between them in an instant.
'Thank you.'

It was so damn polite and civil. Like strangers rather than the old married couple they'd been the hour or so before. Tia had been right when she'd said they'd been like perpetual honeymooners during their marriage. They barely knew each other at all.

He forced himself to resume the tour, to carry on walking through the house and working his way from ground floor to first floor, but the ease between them had gone. Until finally he was opening the door to his study and wondering why they were still fighting a lost cause.

Maybe it would be better tomorrow.

'This is where you work,' she breathed, moving across the space to the huge picture windows in front of his desk. 'You can see a lot from up on this floor.'

'I can watch some of the training exercises without anyone feeling they're being overseen.'

'I imagine you're quite off-putting.'

'Mainly for the clients, not so much my men. They're all ex-soldiers with years of experience.'

'I imagine.'

Again, that restrained stiffness.

'Would you like a drink?' He proffered a decanter of amber liquid, even though he rarely bothered to drink much these days.

For a moment he thought she was going to decline, and then she dipped her head.

'Why not?'

He poured the drinks and then, in silence, they stood by the window and watched Seth—their son—at play with the other children, streaking around the garden and tugging balloons and streamers with them.

'This is what you're reading?' she asked abruptly, breaking the silence. 'First World War books?'

'Autobiographies. From Europe and from the Pacific.'

'I've read this one.' She tapped the cover, her smile sad. 'It's quite moving.'

It would break the fragile bridge if he told her he'd already read it so instead he dipped his head thoughtfully.

'I'll bear that in mind.'

'No problem.'

And there it was, that easiness back. So seamlessly.

They were close, both propped against his desk as they watched the domestic scene unfolding before them. It was all too reminiscent of Tia's consultation room back at the lifeboat house.

And all he wanted to do was to indulge in a repeat performance.

He didn't dare move.

'He has been asking about his father, you know,' she said softly, almost towards the dark edges of the otherwise summer evening.

He waited, but she didn't seem to want to be any more forthcoming.

'What have you told him?' Zeke asked, when he couldn't bear it any longer.

Did Seth think he was dead? Or an absent father who didn't care?

He clenched his fists in anger.

'I told him the truth,' she murmured. 'That is, as much of the truth as I could manage. I told him that his father was a dedicated, loyal, heroic soldier who had won medals for his bravery. But who had been injured in an accident whilst in a hostile country.'

'So he thinks I'm dead.'

A wave of nausea rushed up inside him before Zeke could stop it.

'I don't know,' Tia answered honestly. 'I never said you were, and neither did he. But I suppose he might think that.'

'And when do I get to tell him who I am?'

She turned her head to look at him. The tension between them locking them both into place.

'I don't know,' she half whispered. 'Give me chance to get my head around it all. Everything has happened so quickly these last few days.'

He had meant to lean in closer in some wild attempt to intimidate her, but he really should have known better. Tia—*his* Tia—had never been the type to back down or cower. So, they sat there, his thigh cleaved to hers. Her head tilted, almost belligerently, up to his. Her arms crossed over her chest hinting at her impatience.

And then he saw the faint pulse on one side of her slender neck. Fast, jerky, certainly not as *in control* as she'd had him believing.

It sideswiped him, apparently knocking any last vestiges of sanity from his head. Before he even knew what he was doing, he had snaked an arm out to circle her all too familiar waist, and hauled her to him.

'Zeke...?'

Her hands braced against his chest, her eyes widening, her breath catching.

'Is this what you came here for?' he bit out, as much to deflect as anything else.

How he loved the way her cheeks flushed— as though suffused with guilt. And the way she wanted him, just like back at the lifeboat station, soared through his body, lifting his spirits and soothing his earlier temper. Or, at least, transforming it into something else entirely.

Desire.

'You could have just told me you wanted me to kiss you again,' he taunted. 'To make you come apart the way I always make you. The way you did back in that consulting room of yours.'

'I never gave that afternoon a second thought.'

It was a valiant attempt, but her voice was too breathy. And he knew her too well. A sensation suspiciously like triumph ripped through him. He bent his head to hers, so close the heat from their breath intertwined, and she shivered deliciously in his arms.

'Liar,' he whispered. 'Tell me I never entered your thoughts.'

For a long moment she didn't move. He wasn't even sure if she'd stopped breathing. Her eyes meeting his, darkening, revealing too many things he knew she didn't want them to.

'You came here for more than just Seth.'

His gaze raked hers, hot and greedy and wanting. Then he leaned into her even closer.

'You came to France for the same reason I invited you,' he ground out. 'Because, as dangerous and nonsensical as it seems to be, you and I can't seem to stay away from each other.'

Before she could answer, he bent his head, unable to hold himself back any longer from this burning *need* that threatened to overpower him, and claimed her mouth with his own.

Part of him expected Tia to wrench herself away. Another part of him expected her to slap him. Not a single part of him anticipated her groaning and melting against him as if she really couldn't help herself.

In seconds, Zeke had moved their positions, bringing her around so that their bodies were against each other, his hands caressing her back. And she looped her arms around his neck and pulled herself in tighter, as though she could think of no objections.

As though she thrilled to his touch.

His Tia. His wife. *His.*

He ran his hands down her back, teasing and flirting with the sweet curve of her bottom, pulling her into him so that her heat pressed against where he ached for her most, and it did nothing to help his self-control that all he could remember was the way she had tasted the other day in her office, that glorious scent of her sex, slick just for him, and the way she had come apart so perfectly against his mouth.

'Tia,' he groaned, nipping at the sensitive skin of her neck.

His body howled at him to strip her naked,

spread her out on his desk and thrust all the way home. To have her screaming his name as she had done every weekend they'd managed to snatch together during their marriage, when they'd barely been able to get out of bed most of the time.

The sex between them had never been an issue.

Belatedly, he realised that this was what she'd meant when she'd said they had barely known each other. They'd mistaken unashamed sex for being emotionally vulnerable. But right now, Zeke couldn't bring himself to care. He just wanted to feel her around him, tight and wet, drawing him inside her until he filled her up.

He hooked his fingers under the hem of her cashmere top and hauled it over her head, the sinfully sexy lace bra making his body constrict all the more painfully. And then he spun her around so that his length was nestled between her buttocks as he cupped her breasts with one hand and undid the zip of her trousers with the other.

He heard her murmur of objection, muffled as she let her head fall back whilst he nuzzled the other side of her neck. Arching her back and pressing her breast into his aching palm.

'So good,' he muttered. 'So damn perfect.'

And then he slid his hand into her trousers and

his fingers stroked her sex as though it were the most precious thing he'd ever touched.

The jerk of her hips and her whimper of need was like a lick against his groaning body.

And then just as suddenly as it had begun between them, Tia wrenched herself away. Refastening her trousers and straightening her cashmere top.

Zeke knew what was coming. Was powerless to stop it.

'This can't happen again.'

'You said that last time,' he pointed out nonchalantly, as though her anger couldn't faze him.

'Well, this time, I mean it. We're not kids any more, Zeke. We have responsibilities. I have a son.'

'*We* have a son,' he corrected quietly. Dangerously.

'Indeed you do.' Her eyes flashed just as lethally as she stalked around his study. 'So you should damned well act like it. We're here because you said you wanted to get to know *your* son. But stay away from me, for the rest of this trip.'

CHAPTER EIGHT

'WHAT DO YOU do first?' Tia asked the young lad, her brain fighting to function.

The sun was beating down on them, and with no shade it had already been a long morning of training exercises.

It didn't help that she'd hardly slept in the few nights since that encounter with Zeke. Her mind had been buzzing for days, her body even more so. The worst of it was that, despite everything she had said to him about responsibility, she had imagined going back down to his study and finishing what they had begun.

'Do a blood sweep.' The soldier's voice dragged her back to reality even as he checked down his make-believe patient, moving slow enough to give her time to respond.

'You find blood on his upper-right leg.'

'Check the casualty for holes.'

'You find a gunshot wound,' Tia told him, trying to focus on what was going on around her rather than in her head.

'Okay, I'm going to apply arterial pressure whilst I put a tourniquet around his leg…here.'

'Good—' she nodded '—but you need really solid pressure. Forget your hand, jam your knee right onto it or your casualty is going to bleed out. That's better.'

'How is he doing?' Zeke muttered, coming to stand next to her.

'Okay,' she confirmed, ignoring the way her body pulled tight. As if her skin were too small for her all of a sudden.

'Make sure that tourniquet is really tight. Look.' Zeke moved over to kneel by the trainee, turning up the fabric of his lightweight trousers as he went.

Yet she couldn't help feeling that he had deliberately angled himself so that his body was between her and the bionic limb he was flexing by way of demonstration.

'If my buddies hadn't done that for me, I could easily have lost my whole leg.'

She tried not to take it personally that he didn't mention her part in saving his leg. Or that his voice seemed to be pitched deliberately low. She'd seen and heard him talk about his limb several times to plenty of people over the last few days, but she was sure she wasn't imagining the shift in Zeke's attitude when she was around.

'Tourniquet applied.' The man nodded. 'Checking for other bullet holes.'

'There are no more holes found,' Tia confirmed.

'Does he have radial pulses?'

'He does have radial pulses.' She nodded.

'Okay, I'm calling it in.'

Zeke joined her as she was writing up brief notes and, though it killed her, she leaned over to speak to him confidentially.

'Although he found the gunshot entry point on his casualty's leg, he forgot to turn him over and check for an exit point.' *How could Zeke remain so calm when their arms skimmed each other like that?* 'Also, he never checked for head injuries, or blood in the ears.'

'Mark it down, we'll know to go over it.' Zeke shifted, brushing against her again. Almost more than she could stand.

She took the opportunity to break contact as she circled the trainee and his stand-in casualty.

'You find your casualty is having trouble breathing.'

The trainee paused for a moment before suggesting that his patient was overheating.

Quickly he began to strip his casualty down out of body armour and jacket until he was just in a coat.

'Is that what you were looking for?' Zeke murmured quietly.

'Pretty much.'

'Good. Fine, you seem to have it in hand here. I'll check on the others and then meet you at the house after lunch.'

'Sure.'

She made a mental note to try to avoid the house if Zeke was going to be there after lunch time.

In her peripheral vision she could see him moving away, on to the next team, and concealed her sigh of relief.

If the rest of her month here was going to be this strained then it was going to be hell. But she couldn't give into temptation again, with Zeke.

Zeke stared at the piece of paper in his hand, a whole range of emotions tumbling through him, yet he couldn't seem to grasp hold of a single one of them.

He was still standing in the same spot minutes…weeks…*years* later, when Tia walked into the room. He heard her speak, somewhere in the recesses of his mind, knew she was flustered and apologetic, but nothing registered. Not until she stepped closer, her tone changing to one of curiosity.

'What have you got?'

'A picture.'

'From me,' the lilting, bodiless voice came from the vicinity of the huge brown moleskin office chair. Tia's head jerked and he realised she hadn't even known Seth was in the room, let alone colouring in at Zeke's ornate desk as though it were his own personal colouring station. 'I drew it for him.'

'Oh.'

'It's a rhinoceros,' Seth confirmed, wriggling off the chair. 'I've done another one for Mme Leroy. Can I take it to her?'

She swallowed. Steadied herself, her eyes raking over the picture.

'Sure,' she confirmed after a moment, watching their son leave the room before turning to Zeke, her voice low. 'He loves animals.'

Zeke watched the door close behind the little boy. Marvelled at this incredible person that he—*they*—had created.

'He told me he wants to be a zoo vet, and travel to places like Africa or the Arctic?' Zeke managed.

'Animals have always interested him.' Tia shrugged lightly but he didn't miss the flash of pride in her eyes. 'I don't know if he'll ever become a vet but I'm not about to discourage him.

Ask him about the picture and he'll no doubt tell you that it's a popular misconception that the rhinos' ancestor is the triceratops.'

'He already told me.' Zeke wasn't prepared for the grin that suddenly split his face. 'He was really quite adamant about it.'

'Yes, that's Seth.'

'If I remember rightly, his exact words were that a rhino shares about as much DNA with a triceratops as it does with a human.'

'Did he mention that rhinos actually belong to the same order as horses? That's usually one of his favourite facts.'

It was the lopsided smile that got him. Exactly the same smile that had graced the face of his son only an hour earlier, like a tiny glimpse into the purest of souls.

'He did actually—' Zeke laughed quietly '—alongside a whole host of other facts which he had clearly decided I really ought to know. Then he told me they might have been the original unicorn, so I began to explain that unicorns didn't really exist...'

'I don't imagine that went down well.' She began to chuckle and Zeke's chest pulled unexpectedly tight.

Painful.

How much had he missed that sound over the

last few years? How had he forgotten the way it had always slipped through him, making him feel happy? Contented.

Or maybe that was the point. He hadn't forgotten. He'd merely thrust it aside, locked it in the deepest, darkest pit, and pretended that part of his life hadn't existed. Because he hadn't been sure if he deserved such happiness.

He forced himself to smile. But not to *feel* anything more.

'It didn't. He cast a solemn glance at me and informed me, with what sounded a lot like disappointment, that *obviously* unicorns didn't really exist, but that it was possible that rhinos had been behind the original *myth*.'

'Oh, believe me, I know that tone.' Tia laughed again, a deeper sound, which he couldn't pretend he didn't recognise.

It was surreal.

Five years ago they would hardly have been able to stand in this room together without tearing each other's clothes off. Now they were standing here discussing their son.

Their son.

It didn't seem possible.

'You've done an incredible job with Seth,' Zeke managed, suddenly.

The laughter died on her lips as she chewed them uncertainly.

'Thank you.'

'I mean it. He's a bright, happy, confident little boy. I had no right the other night…threatening a custody battle with you.'

For a moment, she didn't answer.

'I'm sorry, Tia. I really am.'

She still didn't respond, but began to move slowly around the room, dragging her hand over the few trinkets that he allowed to adorn the place. The things that made the place look, if not homely, at least less sparse.

Belatedly, now, he realised they were all items that had been in the home they had once, briefly, shared.

'I'd have thought you would have got rid of these.'

He shrugged but her back was still to him. Probably he should have got rid of them. But he hadn't. What else was there to say?

Because he very much feared that they said too much as it was. That they revealed the sad truth that he hadn't moved on from her, however much he'd claimed to have done. He had a new mansion, a new multimillion-pound business, and a new way to save lives.

But ever since Tia had walked back into his

life, he hadn't been able to shake the unsettling feeling that all these achievements had been little more than him marking time.

Waiting for her.

It was pathetic. Infuriating. And regrettably undeniable.

But the more she looked around his study, his private sanctuary, the more he feared she could read into his heart. Before he could think about it, he heard himself speaking again.

'Come out with me tomorrow tonight.'

Less of a request and more of a demand. At least it made Tia turn, and stop analysing his study.

'To where?'

'The Mayor's Charity Ball.'

She narrowed her eyes, assessing him.

'It doesn't sound like your kind of thing.'

He grimaced.

'Z-Black needs a new permit and the mayor isn't convinced. I could do with a little moral support.'

'Since when do you need *any* kind of support?' Tia asked warily.

There was no reason at all for his heart to be hammering so wildly. Like an adolescent boy asking out his crush for the very first time.

'It couldn't do any harm. It's a nice night out, apparently, and you would be my date.'

In an instant, Tia went from smiling to on edge. 'I… I can't.'

'Why not?' It was as though he could almost taste victory only for it to be snatched away from right in front of him.

'Seth, for a start,' she announced, as though convinced it would satisfy any concerns.

'Mme Leroy would love to babysit for the evening.'

'Right. Well. I don't have a dress. Galas haven't really been high on my priority list the last few years.'

'I'll have someone bring a selection over within the hour,' he countered.

She pursed her lips, leaning her hands on the back of the couch and eying him apprehensively.

'Zeke, is this really such a good idea? Won't people…talk?'

'A married couple attending together. Yes, I can see how that would make the headlines.' He laughed, making her feel foolish despite everything.

'Surely you can't really need me there?'

'I do,' he said simply.

And when she blinked at the uncomplicated emotion in his words, something clenched low in his stomach. He found himself not wanting to give her the chance to back away.

'Go and get ready to collect Seth, Tia, have some time together. I'll set the rest up.'

'I can help for a few moments.'

'Go, Tia,' he growled. 'I'll deal with it.'

And then, before she could argue any more, he strode around the desk, tucked the rhino picture neatly under the glass paperweight on top of his desk, and flicked out his mobile phone, as though his momentum could somehow galvanise Tia, too.

Either way he took it as a small victory when, a few moments later, she turned and headed out of his study.

It felt like less of a victory when he heard his son's shout of delight following a splash and found himself standing at the study window, which overlooked the covered infinity pool, less than ten minutes later, unable to drag his gaze from the sight of his wife stepping out in peacock-blue and executing a graceful dive into the perfectly still waters.

He wanted her with an almost overwhelming intensity.

What the hell was he playing at?

Tia was supposed to be a part of his history, his past. Not something he had to poke at every available opportunity. Like sticking his tongue against a loose tooth when he'd been a kid.

The sooner he remembered that, the better.

'Where's Zeke?' Seth demanded as the two of them headed to the pool together. 'Isn't he coming swimming?'

'No, sweetheart, he had to work.'

'Oh.' Seth peered at her. 'I thought it might have been because he couldn't get his robot leg wet.'

Tia froze, feeling as though her entire body were twisting itself around and around as she turned to her son.

'What do you know about Zeke's leg?'

'Oh, he has one real one and one robot one,' Seth declared. 'Didn't you know?'

'Yes,' she nodded, relieved he clearly didn't know that she had been the one to amputate. 'I did know that, actually. But how do you?'

'I've seen it.'

A gurgle rippled through her. Of course Seth had seen it; Zeke wore shorts out here. It was practical, and suddenly a vivid memory rushed her of the time when, five years ago, the rehab centre had told her to stop worrying about Zeke hiding his leg and give him time, telling her that most of their amputees came to wear their limbs like a badge of honour.

Back then, she'd never believed it would be Zeke.

Every time he'd looked at his legs, he'd had such an expression of loathing. Whether at her for amputating, or at himself for living when his buddies had died, she'd never quite been sure.

It was better than hiding away and feeling somehow 'defective', as Zeke called it.

'Plus, you know, he has taken it off for me.'

Tia snapped her head around to Seth.

'Zeke has taken his leg off for you?'

That was some level of trust. It was ridiculous that she should feel jealous of her son. Or that it rankled so much that Zeke appeared more comfortable to show Seth his amputation than he felt with her.

She tried to shake the foolish notion off, but she couldn't.

'He took it off this morning to show the other kids with robot arms or legs.'

'What other kids?'

'At the sailing school we went to. You remember, Mummy.'

She remembered that Zeke and Seth had been spending some time getting to know each other whilst she was carrying out the medical training that morning. But she'd had no idea Zeke had been planning to take his son to a sailing school. And certainly not that it had been for other amputees. But how utterly Zeke.

It was wonderful that he was bonding with his son, over something he loved so dearly. And it was utterly nonsensical for her to feel excluded.

So why did she?

'I didn't know you were going to a sailing school, that's all.' She plastered a bright smile to her lips. 'I think sailing is a lovely hobby to have.'

'Come with us,' Seth declared suddenly. 'We're going back tomorrow. I think there's going to be a race.'

'I have to lead another medical training exercise,' she realised. 'But Zeke will look after you. Just remember to listen to everything he tells you to do. He's an incredible coxswain.'

'That's the person who steers the ship,' her son told her proudly. 'Zeke explained it to me today. He told me that he set up the sailing school to help children who lost their arms or legs just like he did. Only he was a soldier, Mummy. Like you were. Isn't that cool?'

'Very cool,' she agreed, cranking her tight smile up a notch.

The last thing she wanted was for Seth to think

that she objected to him spending time with his father—not that he even knew that was who Zeke was.

Lifting her hand to her head, she massaged her temples. It shouldn't feel this complicated, and she should be pleased that Zeke was sharing such a vital part of his life with his son, and it was clear he was doing it in such a way that Seth thought it all terribly *cool*. But there was a part of her that felt...*odd*.

As though Zeke was able to open his life up to his son in a way he had never been able to do with her.

Even before the accident.

But surely that was insane?

Still, she couldn't escape the disconcerting notion that he had avoided doing anything with his leg since she had arrived. The way he'd been getting out of his wet gear at the lifeboat station that night. The way he'd been at his house when she'd been there. Even here.

As though he was okay with her seeing it if he was dressed, but that he couldn't let her see him with nothing *but* the prosthetic.

Which was ridiculous, given the way he'd made her orgasm with such wild abandon.

But, as she sat at the poolside, her feet dipped into the cool water, Tia pondered the problem and wondered if tomorrow she might now find a way to pop down to the sailing school and see Zeke in action, after all.

Not that she wanted to get closer to Zeke for her own benefit, of course. But it would be a good thing to do now that he was going to be a part of Seth's life.

CHAPTER NINE

'YOUR LITTLE BOY is loving his time here, isn't he?' Netty, one of the other mothers, laughed as she watched Seth run after her own son, both of them shrieking with delight.

Tia also watched the boys play. Seth and Robbie—who had lost his right arm aged two because of meningitis—had apparently become firm friends in the week they had been together. It was a shame that in a few days Netty would be taking him home, her week-long holiday over.

'Seth adores it,' Tia acknowledged. 'And Zeke loved sharing his passion for sailing with him.'

'So you and Zeke are…?'

Tia paused.

'Zeke is Seth's father, if that's what you're asking,' she admitted.

There was something about Netty that was instantly trustworthy, and Tia hadn't had anyone but her father to talk to in a very long time. And because there was no point pretending otherwise.

Not when the two of them were heads together as they so often seemed to be.

'But…?' Netty prompted gently.

'But…we've only just…reconnected. And Seth doesn't know.'

'Yet.'

'Right.' She gritted her teeth. 'Yet.'

She sensed rather than saw Netty's sympathetic smile.

'You could do a lot worse than Zeke, you know.' Leaning sideways, she nudged Tia softly in the arm, like a show of solidarity. 'There are plenty of women here who have been trying to land him ever since he founded Look to the Horizon a few years ago. Some of them are even married.'

'And Zeke has…been tempted?'

Netty tipped back her head, her rich laughter almost as gloriously warm as the sun itself.

'Never once, Tia.'

'Oh, right.' *It didn't mean anything. It didn't change anything.*

'And before you ask…sure, I've been tempted. I mean, Zeke's set up this charity to show kids like Robbie that they should never be constrained by what society tells them they should or shouldn't do.'

'As Seth would say, setting up this sailing school is *way cool*.'

'Way cool,' Netty agreed. 'But Zeke also teaches these kids a whole lot more than just sailing. He inspires them to be proud of themselves, and he shows them how to stay mentally strong when people are unkind or impose limitations. He defines the very idea of a kind, caring guy and he's one heck of a role model. And let's face it, he's also fit as hell.'

'True,' Tia agreed, baring her teeth in what she hoped looked like a smile.

'Relax.' Netty laughed again. 'I said I've looked. Who wouldn't? But I've never acted. I got the impression that he was closed off to the possibility of relationships. I always suspected that his heart was taken by some special girl. And here you are.'

'Oh, no. No. It isn't like that at all...' She faltered as Netty reached over and placed her hand on Tia's arm.

'Tia, take it from someone looking at the two of you with no preconceived notions. It is *exactly* like that.'

'He hasn't looked this way once.' She would have swallowed the words down if she could have. But they evaded her attempts to capture them. 'He doesn't even know that I'm here.'

'Trust me, Tia. He knows. Now, stay here, I'm going to get us a refreshing drink. It's roasting out here today.'

Tia murmured a word of thanks, her eyes still on Seth and Robbie, who had already raced back to Zeke and were listening attentively to whatever it was he was teaching them.

Emotion banded around her chest.

This was a side of Zeke she'd always wondered about. If it lurked beneath the surface of their tempestuous, stymied relationship. She'd certainly never known it. Maybe it was meeting too young when his own father's lessons had been too close to the surface, or maybe it was marrying as kids where he'd wanted to prove himself the alpha male; either way it came down to poor timing.

He hadn't even told her directly that this charity was his. When she'd asked him about it he'd simply said that when Z-Black had taken off, he'd realised that he had the chance to build something quite special. Not just teaching a few kids a few skills, but teaching them something as challenging as sailing. Helping them to see it less as a disability. Even just assisting them to get the right prosthetics.

Basically everything that Netty had said, only

she'd been full of admiration where Zeke had dismissed his own work.

It was so far removed from the young, arrogant, almost selfish Zeke of old. Like the man she'd always imagined he was, but who he hadn't been. Not back then. He'd been too young. They both had.

Netty was wrong, Tia thought sadly. She didn't have Zeke's heart.

She never had.

It took a superhuman effort for Zeke not to look across the harbour to where Tia and one of the other mothers sat, apparently deep in conversation.

However much he tried to push her out of his thoughts, she was still there. Setting his body on fire just by being in the same house as him. The same country.

He could still taste her, feel her, picture her. The very thought of her took him out at the knees.

He grimaced at his own dark humour.

Bringing Tia and Seth out here had been supposed to have been about him getting to know the son who she had denied him for the past four and a half years. That was certainly what he'd told himself. The truth was that he couldn't drag himself away from her.

He should resent her for those unilateral decisions she had made. Instead, he still wanted her—just as he had five years ago. Ten years ago. Even fifteen years ago.

He still craved her.

And for Zeke that was a weakness that he despised.

Bringing them out here might have given him an opportunity to develop a relationship with his son, but it had also been because a side of him had desperately wanted Tia to see the success he'd made of his life.

That kid from the dirtiest house in Westlake. The kid who her father had tried to keep her away from. The kid she had chosen to marry.

Though he suspected even that had more to do with the death of her mother—grief propelling her to such an emotional act of rebellion—than the fact that she had truly loved him.

She'd been right when she'd told him that she thought they had been more in love with the idea of each other, than they had truly been in love with the people they were.

'Can we show Seth how to rig the boat again?'

Robbie's excited voice penetrated Zeke's

thoughts. Both boys were standing, excited and expectant, in front of him.

'Please, Zeke?' Seth urged, and Zeke wasn't prepared for the longing he felt to hear his son call him *Daddy.*

His son. It was a transformative feeling, this rush of...pride and...love, which poured through him, like nothing he'd ever known before.

'Sure.' Zeke laughed, glad of the distraction. 'Why not?'

It was a good hour before Zeke looked for Tia again. His pulse momentarily accelerated when she wasn't where he'd last seen her—of course she wasn't. Scanning the area, Zeke could only come up empty. She must have gone home without him.

It was ludicrous how let down that made him feel.

He moved around the harbour, interacting with all the kids as he would normally do, Seth and Robbie proudly flanking either side of him. But knowing that Tia had been here and was now gone dampened his mood in a way it surely had no business doing.

He shouldn't expect her to stay; they weren't a family. He didn't know *how* to be a father. He had hardly had a shining example to follow. But he wanted it. He thought he could learn it. Tia might not agree.

The fear clenched at him more than he could have believed possible. A red-hot poker to his belly.

It was only as he crossed the road bridge to the other side that he caught sight of Netty's bobbing head. He had no idea how he managed to make his voice light and easy.

'Have you seen Tia?'

'Hey, boys.' Netty smiled happily. 'I see Robbie and Seth have been having the best time with you, Zeke, so Tia went home. Apparently you have some gala to go to tonight?'

'She left?' He heard the flat tone to his voice, but Netty didn't seem to notice.

'Yeah, she figured Seth was safe with his dad, so she told me she was going to get a shower and get ready.'

'Right.' He nodded on autopilot.

Tia had told Netty that he was Seth's father? It was the first time that she'd told anyone, as far as he knew. His heart thundered in his chest.

'Thanks, Netty.' He reached out for Seth, the little boy confidently gripping his hand.

Father and son.

'Bye, Zeke,' Robbie chanted happily before

turning to his mum, chattering nineteen to the dozen.

Leaving Seth and Zeke to return to the chateau.

Home.

Nothing had quite prepared Tia for the almost overwhelming barrage of yelled questions, cameras shoved in her face, and flashbulbs going off blindingly in their eyes, right from the moment they stepped out of their limousine. She might have known the men of the local chateau would be minor celebrities out here. Especially when they looked like Ezekial Jackson and William Zane.

In spite of a whole week of coaching herself to keep her distance from her estranged husband, she plastered a tight, bright smile to her lips and took comfort from the heat of Zeke's steely body pressed against hers, as she gripped his arm tightly. As if she would never let go.

As if she never wanted to.

Even her body, it seemed, had never been more aware of just how close they were walking. Her pulse tapping out a message, like a Morse code warning. Her radial, her carotid, her femoral. Growing ever more intimate—just as Zeke himself might have managed.

'Just a few more steps.' His deep voice suddenly vibrated sensuously against the skin just in front of her tragus as he leaned down close—perhaps too close—to conceal his words from the plethora of mics and cameras. 'You're doing just fine.'

He shouldn't know her, be able to read her, so damned easily.

'Why wouldn't I be?' Somehow, she managed to up the wattage of her public smile, even as she muttered out a response through her teeth.

When he dipped his head towards her again, amusement threaded through his tone, it was all she could do to supress the delicious shiver that chased right through her.

'Of course, my mistake. Antonia Farringdale is never thrown.'

'It's just a ball.' She had never been so glad to reach the end of a carpet and step through doors that finally, mercifully, restored a degree of anonymity from the press on the other side. 'A party by any other name.'

She braced herself, waiting for Zeke to throw back the fact that they had never really attended parties, balls, or even merely nightclubs together.

Ever.

Not as the young, fresh-faced new Royal Marine and his young, university-bound bride. And not as the battle-hardened, secretive SBS and black ops specialist and his second-in-her-class, rising star of an army trauma doctor wife.

They hadn't had time for partying. Any more than they'd had the contacts for social networking. And she'd never once lamented that fact.

Until now.

Standing, suddenly frozen, on the inside of the huge doors, Tia surveyed the scene in front of her. It was like something out of a fairy tale, either animated or acted, it made little difference. It was breathtaking, spellbinding.

Everything and everyone glittered, from the stunning gowns to the tinkling laughter, as though magic had been sprinkled all over. The whole place seemed brighter than reality, more resonant. The colours richer.

And something permeated Tia in that instant. She felt abruptly supercharged. Even the music seemed to slink across the floor all the way from the ballroom, winding itself around her feet first, insinuating its way up her body, until her blood was pumping to the same, compelling rhythm.

'Dance with me.'

She shook her head instinctively, although the temptation to acquiesce was almost suffocating.

'It wasn't a question,' he censured gently.

But the arm he moved around her waist was less gentle, compelling her to move, to stay by his side as he led them, without another word of objection from her, the length of the hall and around the marble pillars to the ballroom itself.

'I don't know how to dance,' she murmured, even as she walked with him.

'You'll remember. You once told me that you used to dance with your father at Christmas events.'

His voice was even, giving nothing away. Panic began to rise inside her.

'The Zeke I knew didn't know how to dance.'

'Now I do.' He shrugged. 'So I guess all you really need to do is follow.'

And then they were on the floor with his one arm circling her waist, his other hand tucking one of her arms to his chest, drawing her to him, and then there was a jolt and everything... changed.

Tia couldn't move, could hardly even breathe. It took her the longest time to realise that the jolt hadn't been the room, but merely some forgotten, aged electricity that had arced between the two of them.

People were dancing, spinning around them like the multicoloured horses, helicopters and fire engines on the merry-go-round Seth had loved to play on at the park in the last town where they'd lived.

But it was as if she and Zeke were in their own little bubble, right in the centre of them. Staring at each other as if neither of them could work out if they were in their past or their present.

'Are you going to put your other hand on me?' he asked dryly, but there was a rasp to his voice that hadn't been there a few moments ago. 'Or do you intend to dance with your arm dangling awkwardly by your side?'

She didn't answer. She couldn't. She merely lifted her leaden arm and, somehow, placed it on his shoulder.

Even so, it felt surreal when he began moving, leading her smoothly, and she began to follow. As though they had done it a hundred times in the past when the truth was they'd never once danced a ballroom dance together in all their years as a couple.

'Like the waltz we never had,' he muttered unexpectedly in her ear.

'At the wedding celebration that was never ours? We didn't even have a wedding breakfast.'

The words were out before she could swallow them back.

'That's because we had no friends and family to share it with.' His voice lacked any kind of emotion. 'Anyway, we had lunch at the nearest country pub we could find.' He shrugged. 'It was better than burger and fries at the nearest fast-food joint.'

'What the hell were we thinking?' she whispered.

'We weren't,' Zeke answered simply. 'You were rebelling against your father and all his rigid rules. I thought if I had something—someone—back home waiting for me then it meant I would have something to anchor me and keep me safe on every mission.'

It didn't surprise her at all that Zeke never once used the word *love*. So why did it leave her feeling so raw inside? So scraped out.

Perhaps because the truth was, despite his belief to the contrary, she hadn't married him out of some misplaced sense of rebellion. She had married Zeke because she'd loved him. The only man she had ever loved.

Maybe, shamefully, *still* loved, if she was going to be truly honest with herself.

'We were young,' she managed at last, an attempt at an excuse, which she might not like but was infinitely less painful than the contempt and regret with which he seemed to view their marriage.

'Worse. We were idiots,' Zeke ground out furiously. 'You were right that we were selfish and, because of it, you and your father fell out. I pushed you away. But even more unacceptable of all, our son has been fatherless for his entire life.'

She glanced at him, making no attempt to conceal her shocked expression.

'Is that an apology?' she asked at length.

Zeke gritted his teeth. It had always been a standing joke between them that he hated making apologies. He wondered if she'd ever known it was because growing up his father had beat him until he'd apologised for everything. From the lack of food to the fact it was raining on a day his old man had wanted to walk down to the pub.

'It was an observation,' he hedged after the silence got to him.

'It sounded like an apology to me,' Tia muttered, but he could hear the soft smile in her voice. Could imagine the gentle curve of her sensuous mouth.

He locked his jaw even tighter.

'Take it, then. It's the closest you're going to get to one.'

'Then it will have to do. For now.'

It was too revealing. Too intimate. Yet, Zeke still didn't let her go.

If anything, he crushed her all the more tightly until it was almost painful, although she didn't think he was even aware of it. And, perversely, she didn't say anything, as though the pain could numb some of the guilt she'd felt, for too many years.

Irrationally, her eyes began to prickle and Tia dropped her head to Zeke's shoulder before he could see them.

He tensed for a second, but his steps didn't falter, and then they were whirling across the floor together. As a Tia and Zeke from a different life—a parallel universe—might have done.

As though, if they kept spinning and swirling fast enough, hard enough, long enough, they could spin themselves a new history. A different story. It was inevitable that the moment would end. With all the ceremony of a bubble bursting.

'There's the mayor, Jean-Michel Deram. I have to find Zane—we need to put our case forward now.'

She tried not to read too much into the fact that Zeke actually looked regretful to be leaving her. As though he was enjoying this moment between them as much as she was.

Or was she just being fanciful?

'Shall I come with you? Perhaps turning on a little feminine charm would help to lighten the situation, so he doesn't feel ambushed.'

'I'm fairly certain that in Jean-Michel's world

he is accustomed to being *ambushed*, as you call it. But yes, you should come. Thank you.'

And when he looked at her like that—as though they were finally back on the same side when she couldn't remember how they'd got onto opposing sides—she felt as though she were invincible. Just as she had over a decade ago.

CHAPTER TEN

IT WAS ALMOST impossible to keep his mind on business when Tia was sparkling and glowing like that, Zeke realised half an hour later. When he wasn't sure he could recall a single thing he'd uttered since they'd come off the dance floor to put Z-Black's case to Jean-Michel.

She'd known when to hold back when the conversation had flowed, and had instinctively lightened the conversation on the few occasions it had threatened to degenerate into an argument between passion and bureaucracy. All the while keeping them on point, finding a softer way to reiterate whatever point he and Zane had been trying to make a little too forcefully.

Every smile and laugh from Tia seemed to weave a magic spell over their company. She *shimmered*. And he had been wholly unable to drag his gaze away from her. Even when she had excused herself from the negotiations, Zeke had found he was only listening to Jean-Michel with one ear. The other listening out for Tia's tinkling laughter.

He was constantly seeking her out as she moved gracefully through the room, her less than perfect French and evident English accent only appearing to delight the company all the more.

It had started from the moment she'd positively floated down the stairs at the chateau, poured into a dress that was both modest and which made his body tighten so painfully that he wanted to throw her over his shoulder, carry her upstairs to his suite and rip every last shred of material off that sensuous body of hers.

It had continued when they'd been in his expansive four-by-four, which had felt altogether too cramped and suffocating, as the back seat of the car had thrown up all manner of salacious memories from their early marriage that he would do better to forget.

Dancing with her had been a mistake. It had left him hyper-aware of her, and too distracted to focus on the reason he'd even come to this infernal ball in the first instance.

Tia, however, despite her earlier declarations of hating galas and balls, appeared to be the social butterfly of the night. Watching her was mesmerising.

Occasionally a man had got too close, too

hands-on, and Zeke had barely been able to stop himself from asserting himself.

But Tia wouldn't have thanked him for his interference. He could almost hear her voice in his head reminding him that she was perfectly capable of looking after herself.

Only he didn't want her to have to.

And then, suddenly, she turned and smiled at him from across the floor. A dazzling, arresting smile that stopped his heart in an instant. Before he could process what she was doing, she had ducked away from the pawing man, and adhered herself to Zeke's side.

He tried not to let his body react. Fighting the instinct to place a possessive arm around her shoulders. It wasn't him she wanted, it was merely his physical protection from her unwanted suitor.

And then, despite his self-cautions, as the man followed her, clearly not taking the hint, Zeke set his glass down and very slowly, very deliberately, set himself between Tia and her harasser.

He had the sense that half the room was watching avidly, but the man's eyes were still fixed covetously, drunkenly, on Tia and he almost didn't even notice Zeke's unspoken warning.

Almost.

Belatedly, his eyes crossed, and then he jerked

his head back as he tried to look up without stumbling backwards.

Zeke crossed his arms over his chest, knowing it made him look all the more imposing. Finally, the man conceded defeat and, spinning around, marched in a not quite straight line in the opposite direction.

For a moment, Zeke watched him go, and then he turned to his wife, and held out his hand and hoped for her sake that she had the good sense not to object.

In his heart she was still his. *His.* There would never be anyone else for him and, whilst she was with him at this chateau, there could never be anyone else for her.

He couldn't have borne it.

It was weak, and shameful, but he couldn't let her go and he couldn't empty his mind of her since that moment back in her consultation room.

Actually, he had never been able to empty his mind of her since he'd turned up for his first day as a lifeguard only to see her scrubbing down the fibreglass sailboats in those little denim shorts and bikini top she'd favoured all those years ago.

Oh, he'd pretended that he'd got over her—even to himself—but he was beginning to realise just how much of a hopeless lie that had been.

And now here she was again, daring him to be

his own undoing. Making him walk away from the mayor of the town where his livelihood was based—millionaire or not.

Just to be with her.

'So, shall we finish that dance?'

Her whole body might as well have been on fire, the way that Zeke was looking at her. So directly. As though he was seeing her for who she was—and who she used to be—rather than as the doctor who had done a terrible thing to him.

It was a heady experience, crowding in on her and making her feel naked and vulnerable in front of him. Despite everyone else in the room. As though he owned her, body and soul.

Or perhaps that was just the wanton side of her. The one that Zeke—and only Zeke—had always brought out in her. They had been getting so close these last few weeks, almost like they had once been, maybe it was just inevitable.

Her pulse beat out a rapid tattoo onto her skin, as though trying to warn her not to be so naïve. He wanted his son, and keeping her close, keeping her amenable, was a perfect tactic. And Zeke was nothing if not a tactician; his military training had taught him that much. Always thinking three moves ahead.

Well, this time, so was she.

She wasn't going to let Zeke just do with her

as he wanted. She was going to make a few demands of her own. Turn the tables for once and take the lead. Show him that he wasn't as in control as he liked to think he was. At least with her.

She braced herself as he drew her closer to him before telling herself that she couldn't allow him to see how he affected her and instead forced herself to relax into his arms. Forced herself to act as though she were happy to be in his arms. But when his mouth brushed her cheek, she forgot that she was only meant to be playing at it.

He could rescue her. If he wanted to. From a life where she'd resigned herself to never being in love with anyone ever again. From blaming herself for the choices she'd made that night, and the guilt over keeping Seth a secret from him, even though she knew it had been the right decision at the time.

For all their sakes.

Then, as his arm snaked around her back, the heat of his hand searing into the sensitive skin at the hollow of her spine, she watched, transfixed, as his other hand enfolded hers easily. It was all too easy to follow where he led. Floating across the floor as though she were little more than a weightless skein of thread, draped loosely over his arm.

That dark, possessive glint in his eyes shooting

right through her and heating her through to her very core. She lost sense of reality, of where they were, of anyone else in the room. They simply moved around the dance floor together, in flawless synchronicity as one piece of music blended into another and another, with nothing else existing for Tia but Zeke. Her husband, and the father of her wonderful son.

And when the music stopped momentarily, the musicians pausing for a brief rest, and Zeke escorted her off the dance floor, forging a direct path through the hastily parting crowds, she accompanied him wordlessly. But her entire body was alive, exulting in the dark, haunted look in his eyes, which she recognised only too well. She'd seen it many times over the years, but that first time had been the night he'd returned to Westlake—after she'd turned eighteen—and she'd stepped out of the calm, moonlit sea to where he'd been standing over her pile of clothes, a concerned expression clouding his features.

She'd laughed as he'd berated her for going into the water alone, at night, holding his coat out to her in some effort to preserve her modesty, and she had tugged it from his hands and thrown it onto the sand, moments before stepping right up to him and pressing her lips against his. His resolve hadn't lasted much longer.

It had been reckless, and exhilarating. Moulding exactly how the future of their relationship would be.

Possibly she should be more mindful that over fifteen years had passed since that first moment together, and they weren't kids any more. But she wasn't mindful at all. She was only too happy to follow him as he made his way down the imposing hallways, looking for a small, empty room that would suit their needs.

'This will do,' he muttered, poking his head around the fourth door then tugging her inside.

'It will do?' she teased, her laughter floating lightly around them. 'How romantic.'

Zeke rolled his eyes.

'Shut up and kiss me.'

'Willingly,' she agreed, taking one of his hands in each of hers and throwing them around her back as she stepped into the circle of his arms and pressed her lips to his.

Fire roared through her. As he kissed her back, demanding and unyielding as ever, the guttural sound of his approval made desire pool between her legs. He claimed her mouth with his, plundering over and over, using his lips, his tongue, even the rough pad of his thumb, to devastating effect. With no question as to which of them was in control.

She arched against him as if trying to urge him on further, pressing every malleable inch of her lithe body against every muscular, merciless inch of his. But still Zeke seemed determined to prolong her exquisite agony, catching her hands and raising her arms to hold her wrists in one big hand as he allowed his mouth to travel from her mouth to her jawline, but no further.

Tia moved her body, half undulation, half writhe, until Zeke growled at her.

'Be still.'

'I can't,' she gasped, the rawness of his tone scraping deep within her. 'I need more.'

'Then I'll make you.'

Without warning, Zeke crushed his body to hers, trapping her between his solid chest wall and the cold wall behind her. The pressure helping to ease the ache in her straining nipples. And then, finally, he lowered one hand and grazed it over her breasts. Cruelly on the wrong side of the fabric.

'Is this where you want me?' Teasing, taunting. 'Here?'

Tia could only moan and breathe his name. The wild thing inside her clawing its way out.

'Or maybe here?' He skimmed his hand lower over her dress until his knuckles brushed her heat.

'You know exactly where,' she muttered, arching her back then lifting her hips to reconnect with his departing hand.

Instead, she connected with something far more solid, and primal. And Zeke's groan of response galvanised her.

She took advantage of his momentary lack of focus, freeing her hands from his grip above her head and loosening his hold on her. Then, her eyes locking with his, she slowly, deliberately, sank to her knees in front of him.

'Tia...'

'Shhh.' A wicked smile toyed with the corners of her mouth. 'I'm only doing what you did for me barely a few weeks ago.'

Then, sliding her hands to his waistband, she unhooked the suit trousers and drew the zip down in one perfect flourish. It was only as she slid them down his legs, her hands running down the front of his thighs and revelling in the power of the muscles beneath her palms, that Zeke pushed her away from him and took a step back.

'No. This isn't how it's going to go.'

Tia frowned, confused. She stood up and might

have stumbled towards him, if he hadn't looked so hostile.

'What isn't?' she challenged shakily.

'This. You. It isn't going to be like that.'

She blinked, her mind whirring. And then the truth began to dawn, ravaging her as it did.

It was about his leg. What she'd done.

'This is about control,' she whispered, horrified. 'You only want me if you're running the show.'

'That's nonsense.'

'It isn't. You want me to give myself up to you completely, and be vulnerable, but you refuse to do the same for me.'

'Forgive me if I thought I was just trying to make you scream in pleasure. I confess I rather like it when you shout out my name as you come apart against my lips.'

She supressed a sinful shiver at the memories his words ignited.

'Yet when I want to give you the same pleasure, you stop me. Because in your book, that would mean letting me be in control. Opening yourself up to me.'

'You're overthinking this,' he warned.

'Is it that you haven't forgiven me, Zeke?' She forced herself to ask the question even though she feared the answer he might give. 'For cutting off your leg? Or for saving your life when no one could save the lives of your buddies?'

It hung there between them, like an axe just waiting to fall. And then Zeke steeled himself, shutting her out as he always had.

'You don't know what you're talking about.'

The words were too harsh, too brutal.

'Or maybe you still don't quite trust me.' She refused to cry. Even though it nearly killed her. 'You're okay with being with me as long as you're running things. Like the other week. But you don't trust me enough to do the same.'

'It isn't that simple,' he gritted out.

'No, you're right. It isn't,' Tia agreed. 'It's not about intimacy, is it? It's about control. As long as you have it over me, that's okay. But not the other way around.'

She wanted to hear him deny it. Longed to. Even as she knew he couldn't.

'You're right.' He dipped his head eventually, without a trace of remorse.

Tia watched as he calmly adjusted his trousers, her entire body shaking as though from the inside out.

But whatever else they might or might not have wanted to say to each other, it was curtailed by the sound of the announcer on the PA system. Introducing the mayor and beginning the speeches.

'I have to go,' he ground out, smoothing down his suit and stepping past her to the door. 'And so do you.'

The irony of it wasn't lost on Tia.

'I can't.'

'You're my guest. You have to,' he commanded sharply.

'I can't. People will see me. They'll *know*.'

His look was both impatient and regretful.

'They won't see anything, Tia. You look…as stunning as ever.'

She shook her head but he snatched up her arm. Not rough enough that it hurt, but firm enough that she couldn't break free.

'The timing is bad, I'll agree. But…*this* wasn't meant to happen. We will talk about it though.'

She baulked. If she felt this embarrassed, and ashamed, and angry now, how would she feel when the numbing shock had worn off?

'I don't want to talk about it.'

'Well, clearly we need to,' Zeke countered. 'But not now. Later. Tomorrow. We'll go for a walk, show Seth those locks, just like I promised.'

Before she could find another objection, he tugged her to him, ran a hand through her tousled hair as though to smooth it, and propelled her out of the room.

CHAPTER ELEVEN

HOW THE HELL had he let this happen?

He'd been thinking the same thing since he'd stood in front of the rowdy, clapping crowd last night when all he'd been able to see had been Tia. Her face white with shock and her eyes wide with pain.

He should never have taken her to the gala. More to the point he should never have danced with her. Or taken her to that room like the irresponsible teenagers they no longer were.

It was galling that she was right, though. That a part of Zeke either didn't forgive her or didn't trust her. Even though he wanted himself to do both.

Even though he wanted to move on with his life and look forwards.

But it wasn't about his leg, as she assumed it was. It was more about the truth that every time he looked at Seth, this wonderful, glorious, little boy that he had never known he wanted, Zeke felt a rushing loss at the years he had missed out on.

And he couldn't help blaming Tia for it.

The fact her decision to walk away without telling him that she was pregnant had been based on what had happened on that mission that night meant, unfortunately, that the two events were bound up in each other for ever.

'So these works were quite a feat of engineering.' He forced himself to smile at the fascinated boy, who nodded so seriously, sounding out the headers for the tourist information boards, and pointing out the part of the locks that he recognised.

He really was a marvel. His *son*.

Whilst beside them Tia offered a rictus smile and tried to walk as far away from him as she could.

They discussed the works a little longer, with Zeke showing Seth how the series of chains and floodgates would have worked, and Tia moved away, tilting her head up to the sun as though it could conceal the dark shadows on her eyes from lack of sleep, or the lines etched onto her usually smooth features.

And then, finally, they were walking back. Seth skipping obliviously down the dusty canal path, leaving his parents to walk reluctantly together.

'I'm sorry,' Zeke offered at length.

'What for?' He hated that distant, detached quality to her tone. 'For not being able to forgive me, or for not being able to trust me? Or maybe you're only really sorry that I found you out.'

For a moment he didn't answer, and when he did it was more contemplative than anything. The truth only just starting to work its way free in his own mind.

'It isn't about forgiveness,' he began. 'There is nothing to forgive. I know you did the only thing you could when you amputated. If you hadn't then by the time I was flown anywhere else they would have had to amputate above the knee. That's if I had even survived the flight anywhere else.'

'What about your buddies?'

'Duckie and Noel,' Zeke breathed slowly. 'I blamed myself for a long time. You're right—I hated the fact that I was here and they weren't. I wondered what was so damned special about me that I hadn't been killed too.'

'They were just unlucky, Zeke. Desperately, tragically unlucky. It wasn't about you, or them, or anyone else in your squad that night.'

'Logically, I know that. But…you know this well enough, Tia. Logic doesn't always win out.'

'But you *know* it?' she whispered.

'A part of me does.'

'Then last night…?'

'That should never have happened,' he ground out.

The truth was that he suspected it was more to do with *trust* than he had realised. He still sometimes thought of Tia as that young teenage girl, and himself that invincible teenage boy. Whilst he might have long since come to terms with his prosthetic or bionic ancillaries—even learned to embrace them and the new life they had opened up to him—the idea of Tia seeing him as anything less than *whole* still rankled.

Seeing his bionic leg when he was in his everyday environment was one thing, but seeing it in a more intimate setting—when they were about to make love—was something altogether different. Tia was the only person in the world in front of whom he would feel exposed and *less*, if she saw him as he was today.

Yet he suddenly found he couldn't admit to any of it. Because he already knew what her response would be. He knew she would tell him not to be so ridiculous. He could picture her indignation and her frustration; her ponytail would swing wildly from side to side as she emphasised her words. The image made him smile to himself, even as something clenched hard in his chest, like a fist closing around his heart.

She would tell him that, of anyone, she was the person he could trust the most and how he would want to believe her. But he wouldn't.

He couldn't.

Because however much he had achieved with Z-Black, and with Look to the Horizon, he was still the guy who had let her down. And let their son down.

Zeke squared his shoulders, his voice taking on the authoritative tone that had always come to naturally to him, but which felt strained right at this very moment.

'I'm glad you came here, and we had a chance to…iron things out. Before you return to Delburn Bay, we'll agree on our arrangements for the future.'

'Our arrangements?' Tia echoed warily.

'Financial and, more importantly, access to my son.'

'Let me get this straight…'

Staying detached was harder, much harder, than he could have imagined. He was almost grateful as two cyclists suddenly flew around the corner, causing Tia to stop abruptly and Zeke to rush ahead and scoop up Seth.

A split second later Zeke caught sight of the expression on one cyclist's face.

'Get off the path—' he flung Seth to the side, before racing forward as if he could stop the cyclist from mowing down his wife and son '—and get Seth to safety.'

Tia watched in horror as one of the cyclists slumped forward in his saddle and tipped sideways, the bike veering mercifully away from her little boy but then plunging into the canal as the man fell.

A moment ago she'd been almost grateful to them and their breakneck speed, for appearing so abruptly and giving her a moment to collect her scattered thoughts. Last night she'd been angry, and humiliated. She hadn't thought there had been a single thing Zeke would be able to say to her that would have made her feel any better.

But it was what he *hadn't* said this morning that had somehow soothed her soul. He was ashamed of himself, and angry at his own actions. And he was holding back from her, as though it was *him* who needed protecting rather than *her*.

A vulnerability that he had rarely—if ever—shown throughout their marriage. But rather than making her feel safe with a strong man, as she suspected had always been Zeke's intention, it had made her feel shut out, and held at arm's length. He had never let her close enough to see his softer side.

And surely a man so utterly and completely alpha male as Zeke couldn't be dauntless all of the time? Was this a chance to finally get to see the true Ezekial Jackson as he had never allowed her to before? The *whole* man?

Her thoughts had been spinning and whirling so fast all morning. But when he had apologised, stopped talking, she'd seen those shutters slamming down on her all over again, and she'd been powerless to stop it.

She'd grappled for something to say. Anything. But nothing had come.

Now she had a moment's reprieve. She didn't have to think, she simply had to react. Falling back on what she knew best.

Running up the canal path, shouting and signalling to the cyclist who was in front that something had happened to his buddy. And then Zeke sped past her, shouting at her that Seth was safe behind them and shedding his leg moments before he jumped straight into the canal, cutting quickly through the water to where the cyclist was already sinking below the surface.

Spinning around, Tia watched as her son ran up to her, fascinated and not in the least bit afraid.

'Go on, Mummy, you're a doctor. You and Zeke have to save that man's life.'

With a rush of love, Tia turned to obey.

'The walls here are too steep. There's no way to climb out. Get a rope, or anything to help pull us up,' Zeke yelled as he ducked down to pull the man's head above the water.

It took Tia all of two seconds to locate the nearest moored boat and race across the uneven ground to where its owner was sunbathing, oblivious, on deck. It felt like an eternity as they located a spare rope.

And then Tia was racing back, the other cyclist now lying face down on the edge of the canal, leaning down in a futile attempt to reach his buddy and Zeke—who was doing an incredible job of treading water with the casualty—and help pull them out. But the walls of this part of the canal were too high, and it was clearly proving impossible.

'Grab the rope,' Tia shouted, tying one end around a tree and locking it off before looping the other end and throwing it to Zeke and commanding the second cyclist. '*Aidez-moi*...um... *tirer.*'

With a last, anguished look at his friend, the

man jumped up and hurried over to her, taking hold of the rope between Tia and the canal. His impatience was almost palpable as they both waited for Zeke to finish dropping the loop over his casualty and tie it in place.

'Okay,' he signalled at length, still holding the man's head above water as Tia and the second cyclist began to pull.

It felt like hours but was probably a minute or less before they'd successfully pulled the unresponsive casualty onto dry land, Tia's fingers fumbling to loosen the knot and release the loop for the rope to be thrown back to Zeke.

He couldn't tread water for ever and there was no other way out of this section, but she was going to have to trust the second cyclist to help Zeke. She needed to concentrate on her patient, who she had now ascertained was having a heart attack. There was no choice but to start chest compressions.

'J'ai appelée au secours.'

A strange voice broke Tia's thoughts, and it took a moment for her to realise that it was the woman from the boat.

'I am calling ze help services. They come now.'
'Thank you. *Merci.*'

'Je peux faire quelque'chose d'autre?'

For a moment Tia's head swam, but whilst the

words meant little to her the tone was clear. The woman wanted to help. She continued with her chest compressions.

'Defibrillator?' Tia asked, then, hopefully, *'Défibrillateur?'*

'Non, mais il y a un poste de pompage... How you say? A pump-house? Wait... I go.'

Before Tia could answer, the woman had hurried away and she was left with her patient, not even daring to lift her head to check if Zeke was all right. Or her son.

'Seth, baby, are you all right?'

'Yes, Mummy.' Clear, confident. Trusting her.

She couldn't let this man die. Not for him. But also, not in front of her son.

And then, suddenly, Zeke was there, his voice low and reassuring to Seth. And at the same time the woman was back, mercifully with a defibrillator in her hands. Gratefully, Tia took it and turned to Zeke.

'He's having a heart attack. You take over the chest compressions whilst I get this ready. Okay, stand clear.'

It took two shocks and some more CPR before the cyclist's heart was back in normal sinus rhythm, having managed to converse briefly, and laboriously, with his fellow cyclist. Still Tia was grateful when the emergency services arrived as she was stabilising him, the handover going much smoother when Zeke stepped in to translate, a proud Seth tightly gripping his hand.

Father and son. Her chest tightened, almost painfully. She was at serious risk of falling in love with Zeke all over again. And that would be the definition of stupidity, since it was clear he was every bit as determined to keep her at a distance as he had ever been.

The sooner she got her and Seth back to Delburn Bay, the better.

CHAPTER TWELVE

WITH A FINAL intake of breath to quell her nerves, Tia pushed open the anteroom door to the master suite and stepped inside. The odd noises had stopped a while ago, but the draw was still powerful.

In front of her were the panelled double doors to the bedroom, slightly ajar, to her left a single, open panelled door to his walk-in closet. Tia turned to her right where another single, panelled door barely muffled the sounds of a shower.

Tia froze. *This wasn't what she'd bargained for.*

She couldn't have said how long she stood there, unable to move, but suddenly the shower was being turned off and there were sounds of movement inside. She turned awkwardly, almost crashing into the burr walnut table as she tried to leave.

The en-suite bathroom door opened instantly.

'Tia.' He sounded taken aback and she spun

back around, an apologetic smile plastered on her lips.

'Zeke...'

Suddenly any hostility that she'd sensed in Zeke dissipated.

'Is Seth okay?' he asked urgently.

'Seth's fine,' she managed.

But any other words were choked off by the sight of him standing—filling—the doorway, imposing and autocratic as ever despite his state of virtual undress.

Her mouth seemed to simultaneously dry up and yet water. Her eyes wandering greedily over the sight in front of her, from his wet hair, slightly spiky from the shower, to the broad shoulders that seemed to stretch from one door jamb to the other. One muscled arm was braced against the wooden frame, emphasising his solid, honed, tanned chest, which boasted more of an eight-pack than a six-pack, and which tapered to an athletic waist with hips barely holding onto a towel.

'Is he having nightmares?'

She couldn't have said what it was in the question that made the hairs on her arms prick up but it was suddenly as though a fog were beginning to clear in her head.

Nightmares.

Why hadn't she realised it before? She, of all people, a former army doctor.

Tia blinked, trying valiantly to drag her gaze away but she couldn't. Her eyes were locked onto him as though her brain was fervently trying to memorise every last glorious detail to savour for the future.

'Seth is absolutely fine.'

Zeke seemed to relax a little.

'He isn't upset in any way?' The note of urgency had reduced to one of concern. But it was there, nonetheless. 'He's only a kid. It can't have been easy seeing that man have a heart attack in front of him. It's a shock the first time you see arms windmilling like that.'

'Seth isn't upset,' she reassured him. 'We made sure he was far enough back, and I think you and I both kept instinctively putting ourselves between him and the casualty. I don't think he really saw anything at all. If anything, he seems proud.'

She couldn't move; his scanning gaze was rooting her to where she stood. As though he was trying to work out if she was telling him the truth.

'I'm glad.' Eventually he bobbed his head. A curt, sharp movement that belied his words. 'Thanks for letting me know.'

'Right.' She nodded, hesitating for a moment. 'I should go.'

'You should.'

Neither of them moved. Instead Tia stared, her eyes raking over him again and again, indulging and absorbing. And then they travelled lower. Over the short towel that barely covered his powerful thighs, and down his legs.

Until she could see the one thing he had seemed so hell-bent on keeping from her. The knee and the residual limb. Once she had seen it, she couldn't tear her gaze away.

This was what she had done. Her first ever solo amputation. On her husband. The professional part of herself noted that it had been a good, neat job. The rest of her went hot, then cold, then hot again.

'Seen enough?' His sharp voice pulled her back to reality as he snatched up a temporary crutch from behind the doorway and moved swiftly, smoothly, across the anteroom to where she hadn't noticed an older prosthetic limb by the wall.

Tia watched, transfixed as he slid the liner on, then the fibreglass shell complete with a sleeve art that was so typically Zeke she felt a rush of nostalgia, before he stood forward until the pin fixed into the lock. The click seemed to reverberate around the room, making her jump.

'Where's your bionic limb?' she asked hesitantly.

He paused, as though he wasn't going to answer, then met her gaze and held it. Almost challenging her.

'I wanted to give it a quick clean and check after this afternoon.'

'Right.'

'So, now you've satisfied your curiosity, I suggest you go. Get back to *our* son.'

'Show me.'

The words were out before she could stop them. Zeke's face hardened, his eyes narrowing.

'You want me to show you?'

'Show me how it works.' She nodded. 'You seem to have no problem showing the kids at your charity, or even showing Seth. And I've heard you've turned it into a puppet show at one point to make them all laugh. But whenever I'm around it's different. You shut down, keep me out.'

'You're really making this about you?' he accused her, and for a moment she almost backed down.

But then she remembered that was what Zeke

always did: turned it around on others. It possibly worked well in some of his missions.

It wasn't going to work on her. Not any more.

'No, Zeke. I'm making this about you.' She refused to let her eyes slide away. 'The reason I came down here was because I was checking on Seth when I heard noises.'

'Noises?'

She didn't imagine the way his body stiffened up.

'I didn't realise what they were at first but something about them compelled me to come and check it out. It brought me to your suite.'

'Strange?' He cocked his head as though listening out. 'But I don't hear anything now.'

'No,' she agreed. 'But then we wouldn't. Given that you're now awake. You were having a nightmare.'

'You don't know what you're talking about,' he scorned, but the edge to his tone told Tia everything she needed to know.

'You have them a lot. I should have realised. Have I...? Does me being here make it worse?'

'No.'

But he'd paused a fraction too long and she didn't believe him. She told him so.

'No,' Zeke repeated. More firmly this time.

Tia shook her head sadly.

'I heard you. That was what the noise was, wasn't it?'

He glared at her, yet there was something about his expression that was less hostile than she might have expected. Still, she was shocked when he dipped his head in acknowledgement.

'Yes. I had a nightmare. A particularly bad one, I admit it. But…' He tailed off.

Her heart twisted and knotted inside her chest. There was no way she could leave it that way.

'But what, Zeke?' She waited but he didn't answer. 'You accused me of making this about me and I told you I was making it about you. I want to amend that. I'm also making this about us.'

'This has nothing to do with us,' he said coldly. 'There isn't even an *us.*'

It hurt far more than it had a right to. Still Tia refused to back down.

'At some point you're going to have to deal with what happened. We have a son together, and we're going to end up being in each other's lives for good whether you like it or not.'

'I'm well aware of that, Antonia. It's why I brought you out here.'

'You say there's nothing to forgive, yet I don't feel forgiven. It's like every time we take three steps forward somehow your leg gets in the way and we take another two back.'

Belatedly, she realised what she'd said. She opened her mouth to apologise, astounded when a low chuckle reached her ears.

'Pun intended?'

The tension in the room eased instantly. Zeke always had liked a dark sense of humour. She remembered them telling her at the rehab centre that the lads would rag each other mercilessly. Fellow amputees dismantling each other's chairs and hiding the parts or pushing each other around to see who would topple over first.

She'd been horrified, but the response had been that they didn't take it as bullying, they took it as character-building. The kind of camaraderie they had been accustomed to in their units. It was different in the medical corps, but she could see exactly what they'd meant. Why being in that centre had been far better for him than coming home.

But now, if she wanted to finally reach him, then she was going to have to stop being Tia, his estranged wife and mother of his son. And be Tia, a fellow soldier who took no bull.

'I'd like to say I'd intended the pun,' she hazarded, 'but I'm afraid not. I'll think of a better one for next time, though.'

He watched her a moment longer. Intently, as though he was trying to read her very soul. If she'd known how to open it up for him, then she certainly would have.

'Did you blame me for amputating your leg and thereby keeping you alive, when your buddies had died, Zeke?'

He eyed her again, and then, to her surprise, he smiled. A half-apologetic smile, but a smile nonetheless.

'Maybe. I don't know. When I look back on it, nothing I thought back then was rational, so it's possible. I knew I'd pushed you away but a part of me was still angry that you went. I know now that you called the hospital for updates and that you never expected me to discharge myself and go off grid. Just as I understand why you kept the pregnancy from me initially, and I believe you that you intended to tell me as soon as you thought I could handle it. But that's the part that really gets to me. That you thought I couldn't take it. That you thought I was somehow *less*.'

It tore into her chest, squeezing her heart painfully.

'I never, ever considered that you were less of anything.' Her voice cracked but she forced herself to continue. 'You were…*are*… Zeke Jackson. How could you ever be less than that?'

'You wanted to get away from me, Tia. I saw it in your eyes. You keep trying to deny it but I know it was there, just as we keep trying to move on, but it always comes back to that.'

And then she deflated, right there in front of him.

'You're right. I'm sorry, and I hate myself for it, but you're right.'

The noise that escaped his throat was almost animalistic. Like a roar and a pain, all in one.

'But I *can* tell you that it wasn't about the accident, or the leg, or anything like that,' she pushed on. Desperately. Forcefully. 'Not for a second.'

'Then what, Tia?'

'It was about the fear of losing you. The way I had lost my mother. It had always been there, in the back of my mind, but I'd never once imagined that you would be brought to my camp, on my operating table, with no other choice but to perform surgery on you. It's the worst situation to ever be in, Zeke.'

'I can't imagine,' he murmured, and somehow that soothed her.

'I felt so responsible and so lost. You were lying there, bleeding out, and I froze for a moment. I had no damned idea what to do. And in that moment—as ludicrous as it might sound to you, I wanted to shout and scream and rage at you, for putting yourself at risk and putting me in that position.'

For a moment he didn't speak, so many emotions chasing over his rugged features that she could barely keep up, even though she tried. As if he was weighing up her words. Assessing her sincerity.

The silence felt almost suffocating. Tia wanted to shift, to move, to break free. Yet simultaneously she didn't even want to breathe if it risked breaking this spell they seemed to be under.

And then, after what felt like an eternity, he finally answered her.

'You felt powerless,' he said slowly. 'I understand how debilitating that is.'

She didn't want to have to answer him, but she made herself.

'The prospect of losing you was horrific, and then, on top of that, it opened up everything I'd stuffed down and refused to deal with when my mum had died. I thought I could run away, escape it, let it bury itself again.'

'You thought if you could get away from me in that hospital, then you could isolate yourself from everyone and never get hurt again.' His voice was gravelly. Hoarse.

'How stupid, how *selfish*, was that?' She choked back an angry sob, only for Zeke to cup her cheek.

His thumb grazed her jawline, rough, almost assailing. Silencing her.

'It was understandable. Brave, even. Because you didn't pretend we could be something that we weren't. Not back then. You were right not to have told me straight away about the baby. I would never have given myself a chance to heal. I would have felt pressured to provide for you and I would have made both our lives miserable when I couldn't do it.'

'Zeke—'

'I only regret leaving before you had a chance to tell me.' He cut her off as if she hadn't even spoken. 'I thought I was sparing you the burden of me. But I think it was just a way to run away whilst pretending to myself that I wasn't.'

'The survivor's guilt?' she guessed.

He drew in a breath.

'Yes.'

This was it. This was their chance. Zeke was talking to her; she couldn't blow it. And with Zeke, directness was going to be key.

'You know that's the goal, don't you? That's why they make those IEDs exactly the size they do.'

'Of course I know that, Tia.' He exhaled, but this time there was no rancour in his tone.

If anything, she might have even thought there

might be a touch of relief in it. But that didn't make sense; he had army buddies—both fellow amputees and not—to talk to.

Could it really be relief at finally being able to talk to *her*?

'I run a company that sends men out there in a private role every day. It's my job to know that. Those IEDs are designed to maim, not kill. If you have someone with their feet or legs blown off, screaming their heads off in pain, it not only ties the men up, but it demoralises too.'

'Is that what the nightmare is?' she asked quietly. 'Hearing the screaming?'

His jaw was locked so tightly she couldn't stop herself from reaching out and cupping her palm against it.

She wasn't prepared when he suddenly lifted his arm and covered her hand with his own.

'Sometimes,' he told her, his voice thick with emotion. 'Sometimes it's the silence. And that can be worse.'

Tia couldn't speak.

'Sometimes it's me being blown up. Sometimes I dream that I'm fine, that I was never blown up, but that I'm standing over someone knowing they're dead. Sometimes it's Duckie, sometimes it's Noel…' He hesitated, but made himself push on. 'Or, when things get really rough, the nightmare is that it's *you.*'

'Me? I wasn't even there.'

'But I lost you all the same.'

'I'm sorry,' she whispered eventually. 'I should have realised. I should have…stayed away.'

His hand, still pressed to hers, held her all the tighter.

'The nightmares aren't worse since you reappeared, Tia,' he choked out. 'I hadn't really considered until now, but they've been getting easier over this past month. That one tonight is the first one I've had since you've been back in my life.'

She tried to contain the joy that leapt to life in her soul. But it was impossible.

'Surely that's good?'

'I usually have at least one bad dream every ten days or so.'

So his nightmares were less since she'd come back into his life.

Tia found that she couldn't focus her mind. Her mind might as well have been stuck inside a hurricane and altogether too many questions were screaming around in there.

The world was shifting around her, shimmering faintly, as though it might be full of possibilities after all. The grip on her hand now tightened, almost painfully. Or perhaps that was the grip on her heart.

It was time to move them forwards. As a couple.

Sliding her hand out from between his palm and her jaw, she led him to the small settee in the room and forced herself to smile.

'Show me,' she murmured, letting her hand sweep over his limb. 'Teach me how it works.'

'Tia,' he berated. 'You know how these things work.'

'Not really.' She shrugged. 'I worked at the other end of this process.'

'The cutting end?' He grinned wryly.

She pulled a rueful expression.

'Show me, Zeke.'

'No. It's too jarring,' he vacillated. 'Hardly... romantic.'

She smiled. A soft teasing smile that she could see twisted inside him.

'So now we're being romantic?'

'Aren't we?' he challenged playfully, and the shimmering hope inside her grew incandescent.

'I guess we are.'

'Then how is showing you my prosthetic, or even my stump, romantic?'

She placed her hand on his thigh where it touched hers, trailing a path down to his knee.

'You still don't see it, do you, Zeke? It's romantic to me.'

'I don't believe that.' He shook his head.

'I know. And that's what makes you an idiot,' but there was no rancour in her words. 'But, for the first time in my life, I would feel like it made you *my* idiot. That you were finally letting me in. That, at last, there were no barriers built between us.'

Tia had no idea what it was—whether her words, or her touch, or maybe just the way she was looking at him—but suddenly everything simply...changed. It was as though he had finally decided to try trusting her and all the tension, all the pain of the last few weeks just dropped away.

It didn't matter any more.

There was just her, and Zeke. And she knew he wanted to be with her in the way she'd been dreaming of for years. As long as he knew that she wanted to just accept him for all that he was, in a way that no one else ever had done in the past.

More importantly, he would need to *want* her to.

She waited, her breathing choppy, loaded. For a long time she couldn't be sure it was even going to happen. And then abruptly he pressed his forehead to hers, deliberately, roughly, as though, if they could merge as one, she could understand for herself all the things he couldn't easily articulate.

She didn't know what had changed, but she rejoiced that it had.

CHAPTER THIRTEEN

'Do you know that these last few weeks have been the first time you've ever really begun to talk to me about your mother, Tia?'

'I'm not sure that's true.' She frowned, knowing that it was.

'It is,' Zeke confirmed. 'You have talked about me shutting you out, but it hasn't just been me. I think that was why we were first drawn to each other all those years ago. We each saw a dark void in the other that we pretended being together could fix. We were both running from our pasts but being together allowed us to act as though we were running *towards* something.'

'Maybe we were.'

'We weren't. You would never have married me if you hadn't been desperate to plug the hole your mother's death had left. Just as I wouldn't have talked you into eloping if I hadn't been trying to prove to myself that someone could want me. Love me.'

She wanted to deny it, but deep down she knew he was right.

'So we did it for the wrong reasons, and we messed things up in the middle. But it brought us Seth. There can be nothing more perfect than our son, surely.

'Tia, I'm trying to say...'

But she didn't want to know what he was trying to say. She couldn't overcome the unsettling suspicion that it was going to be something she didn't want to hear. Something that might threaten the possibility of them becoming a family, at last.

Grasping his waist with her hands, she angled her head until their lips just brushed, praying that he would meet her halfway. If she couldn't talk him into trusting her, then she was just going to have to show him in the most primal way she could.

For a long moment, he didn't respond. She could feel his warm, ragged breath, tickling her lips, but they were both frozen there. Paralysed.

And then, just as she thought he was going to move away, he kissed her. A kiss to launch a rocket booster into space. And Tia poured everything she was into that kiss. A long, slow burn that unfurled right through her and scorched her from the inside out. Delicious and destructive all at once. She should stop it. But she didn't want to even try. So, instead, she wound her arms around his neck and pressed her entire body against his. Her breasts splayed against his chest, her thighs nestled between his, and Zeke pushing against her belly, so sinfully hard where she was achingly soft.

She rocked against him, slowly and deliberately, revelling in the low growl that escaped his throat, recognising the familiar, mad heat that surged though him, making his whole body tauten against hers. And then she tilted her head, angling for a better fit, and repeating the kiss between them.

Zeke resisted for one moment more, and then…he stopped fighting her. And it was like unleashing a tsunami. His hands cupped her jaw, he deepened the kiss and he merely *took*. Demanded. Whilst Tia gave herself up to him completely.

His mouth plundered hers, feasting on her as though he couldn't get enough, making her dizzy with a feverish longing. She had no idea how long he kept kissing her, his hands cradling her face then tangling into her hair, sweeping down her back, then grazing up her chest until she was arching wantonly into him.

'Lift up,' he commanded huskily, and when

he cradled her backside, instinct made her raise her legs to wind around his hips, shivering as he pulled her so deliciously onto him.

Velvet against steel.

He carried her across the room and to the bed, lowering her down and covering her body with his own, the molten expression in his eyes scorching her from the inside out. Her body shifted over the bed, and her heart thundered in her ears.

Zeke wanted her. Every bit as much as she wanted him. And the mere anticipation was enough to make her begin to lose herself. To wonder, somewhere on the edges of her consciousness, if she would make it out alive this time.

As if he could read her mind, Zeke bent his head and drew one aching nipple into his mouth, like a shot right from her breast and through her body to her very core. He grazed his teeth over the sensitive skin before sucking on it deeply, intense pleasure and exquisite pain all at once.

Tia lost herself completely.

There was nothing but her and Zeke. The way it had been a decade earlier, before real life had begun to get in the way and over-complicate things. When they had let their hearts rule their heads, and when they had acted on glorious impulse and eloped.

When they had simply felt love.

Still, his mouth, his hands, teased her. Tracing whorls over her bare skin, almost reverently, as though he was taking his time to relearn her. Perfect and intoxicating. And every time he teased her, grazing his teeth over her with just the right balance between gentleness and roughness, a fresh jolt of lust clutched at the apex of her legs.

'It's been five years,' she groaned softly. 'Don't you think that's long enough to wait?'

'It's been *over* five years,' he corrected, his hoarseness betraying him. 'I don't intend to rush this like I did back at the lifeboat station.'

Before she could answer, he moved over her again, shedding the last of her clothes and dropping hot, lingering kisses down between her breasts, to her belly button and lower. Much lower.

The storm that had been building between them ever since that first moment in her new office back in Delburn Bay closed in on her with lightning speed. Only that time, Zeke had been in control. Now she was determined that it would be her.

Not just because she wanted to. But because she *had* to. She had to prove to Zeke that she'd meant what she'd said when she'd told him she hadn't cared about his lost leg. That he wasn't any less of a man to her. He never had been.

With a superhuman effort she pressed her hands against his chest.

'My turn,' she whispered, pushing him away and onto his back. Savouring the fact that he let her.

And then she was astride him, her hands acquainting themselves with every solid, contoured muscle of his chest and stomach, as impressive as it always had been. Her mouth following suit, she took her time, letting her hair slide over his skin until he was scarcely able to conceal the way even those defined edges quivered slightly for her.

Carefully, deliberately, Tia worked her way down to his waist, stopping short at the low band where his towel still clung to his hips. He was ready for her, beneath it. Excitement rippled through her. She felt almost wild. But this was about more than just the sex. This was about proving something to him, as well.

Edging backwards, she moved down his legs until she was at his ankles.

'What are you doing?' he demanded gruffly.

'Shh, just wait,' she murmured, meeting his gaze, holding it.

Without breaking eye contact Tia reached up and curled her fingers around the sleeve art, rolling it down with all the reverence that she might have rolled a condom onto his proud, unabashed sex.

'Tia...'

'Trust me?' It was meant to be a command, but it came out more as a soft plea.

Zeke paused, his eyes narrowed a fraction, before offering an almost imperceptible inclination of his head.

Tacit acquiescence.

Still staring into those fathomless blue depths, she reached for his ankle piece and disconnected it, lowering it softly to the floor beside the bed.

'Now what?' he growled, the undercurrent of anger palpable in his tone.

But she was beginning to recognise Zeke again. Finally. And she knew it was more anger at himself, at the discomfort and uncertainty he was feeling right at this moment, than it was directed at her. So it was her job to eradicate it.

He had trusted her this far, anyway, and that was all the encouragement she needed.

'Now...' a seductive smile pulled at the corners of her mouth '...we play.'

Before he could say anything more, Tia moved

back up his body, and unhooked the towel, letting it fall either side of his hips, her breath catching in her chest as she finally broke eye contact and let her eyes skim down his incredible body to where he stood, so powerfully male.

She swallowed once. Twice. He was every bit as magnificent as she remembered.

Better.

And he was all *hers.*

It was all she could do not to claim him immediately.

Pressing her lips to his inner thighs, she worked her way, higher and higher, determined not to rush, however much she wanted otherwise. However much she had to taste him, *needed* to.

She jolted when he caught her upper arms with his strong hands, stopping her.

'Tia.' His voice was clipped, raw. 'You don't have to do this.'

'This is exactly your problem, Zeke,' she managed, her husky voice alien even to her. 'You refuse to believe how much I *want* to. Even when the evidence to the contrary is right in front of you.'

And then, before he could object any further, she lowered her head and took him into her mouth.

* * *

He was dying.

There was no other way to describe it. This unparalleled pleasure that crashed over him, and all around him.

Her mouth even hotter, cleverer, wickeder than he remembered. And even more urgent than it had been in every one of the futile fantasies he'd harboured in the years since they'd been apart, even whilst he'd thought they would never be together again. As if she, too, had been waiting for this moment. As if she couldn't get enough of him.

She licked him, tasted him, sucked him. The sweetest torture he had ever known. And he could do nothing but lie back and let her, watching her head move over him, letting his fingers tangle in that glorious mass of silken hair of hers. Letting her have her way. Letting her do what she wanted to him.

Tia. *His* Tia.

Claiming him as though she had every right to do so. Turning him inside out. He was building fast. Maybe too fast. Rolling through him like a tornado, a vortex that he couldn't hope to control.

Without warning, she moved her hands to circle his base, her teeth grazing him with the exact amount of pressure before taking him deeper again into her mouth, and Zeke couldn't curb it any longer.

It was like being strapped to a slingshot ride that Tia had suddenly released, leaving him catapulting into space. Crying out her name and who knew what else, as he was shot into a million glorious pieces.

When he came back to himself she was still astride him, watching him. Undisguised victory in those stunning, sparkling eyes. A smirk tugging at one side of her mouth.

'Witch,' he breathed when he could finally speak.

'Why? Because I've just exposed your claims that you have no feelings for the lies they are?'

He could have hurt her. He could have told her that sex and feelings weren't the same thing at all. But suddenly, he didn't want to. He didn't want to dance this power tango any more. He didn't want to fight. He just wanted her.

His Tia.

'Because you have me under your spell,' he muttered, snaking his hands out to hold her as he twisted on the bed so that she was on her back and he was over her. 'Just like you always did.'

Her eyes widened, then darkened.

'Prove it,' she challenged softly, but he didn't

mistake the faint quake in her voice, as though she was half frightened.

'Oh, believe me. I intend to.'

He nestled himself between her legs, his mouth finding that sensitive hollow at the base of her neck, which had her arching her back and making the kind of sounds that instantly reignited the insane fire inside him. But he forced himself to take his time, his tongue licking at her salty skin, his hands following the luscious, fascinating curves of her body. Even when she wrapped her long legs around his waist so sensuously, so enticingly, he refused to capitulate.

Carefully he slid his hand down her body, between them, his slightly calloused hand deliberately grazing her soft skin. Tracing patterns and whorls, indulging and teasing.

Slowly, so slowly, he let his fingers creep down, three finger-walks down, then two back up, heightening Tia's anticipation, until she was moving impatiently under him, her breath coming in short, sharp, little gasps.

He moved down over her belly button, the soft swell below, and finally into the neat hair beneath that. All the while, Tia lifted her hips, turned them, in an attempt to get him to touch her where he knew she ached for him most.

Still Zeke teased her. Toyed with her. And himself. Only when he thought she could take no more did he let his fingers inch lower. Lower. To circle all that slick, inviting heat, around and around. To play with that proud button, with long, slow flicks. To slide inside her where she was hot, and swollen, and waiting for him.

Driving her closer and closer to the edge.

He could see the wave reaching its peak inside her. He relished in it.

'Not like this,' she cried suddenly, trying to twist her hips away from him. 'Not this time.'

'Relax.' He lowered his head to her breasts. To the pink, straining buds.

She cried out, then caught herself again.

'I want more, Zeke,' she repeated. 'I want *you*.'

'I'm here,' he growled, deliberately misunderstanding her. Sucking on her nipple until she was arching up to him again.

'You know what I mean,' she managed, her voice sounding thick, far away, but succeeded in moving her hands down his back to grasp his backside, to pull him to her until his length was pressed against her.

And how he wanted to drive his way inside. Zeke had no idea how he held himself back.

'Say it,' he commanded in a voice he barely recognised.

'You know.' Her head gave a jerky little shake of disbelief.

'Say it. If you really want it.'

'I want you…' She bit her lip shyly. But then, suddenly, a spark leapt into her eyes.

A flash of the old Tia he had lost so long ago. *His* Tia. His *wife*.

'I want you, Zeke, inside me.' Clear, sexy, sure. 'So deep that I don't know where I end and you begin.'

It was like a lightning bolt through his entire body. The words he hadn't expected to ever hear from her again. And he couldn't deny her. He moved so that he hovered at her entrance for a moment, then thrust inside.

Long, deep, hard. Whilst his Tia cried out and lifted her hips to meet him, tightening around him as though to draw him in all the more. He held her tightly to him, withdrawing slightly only to drive back inside her, again and again, until they were both tied up in knots and he didn't think he was going to be able to last much longer.

She was exquisitely perfect. Matching him step for step in this raw, primal dance.

Her body began to tense beneath him, to pull around him, and he reached down between them one more time, and found the hard little bud. This time when he thrust his way home, he flicked his finger and pressed down, and she screamed out his name.

And when she finally hurtled over the edge, falling and tumbling, and shattering into nothingness, he let go and toppled into the blissful abyss with her.

CHAPTER FOURTEEN

THE LIFEBOAT BOUNCED through the heavy seas, every member of the crew on the lookout for the missing yacht.

Given the crashing waves, it was understandable how his antenna had likely been damaged, but it meant locating him was going to be a problem. The search and rescue helicopter was on a shout but had confirmed they would come and help with the search once they were freed up.

Still, Tia thought, peering through the windows, time was going to be a factor, and even though the skipper of the yacht had activated his distress beacon, no one knew what state he was going to be in by now.

'Think I've got him,' a shout went up and Zeke turned the lifeboat in the appropriate direction.

The past couple of weeks had been amazing. Better than anything Tia could have dreamed of, back in France.

Their last week at the chateau had been glorious. Working in the mornings, then being a family afternoons and evenings. Sometimes going together to Look to the Horizon, other times simply going to a local market, or a show, or even just the beach.

Then this week back at Delburn Bay had been wonderful. It had been tempting to move in with Zeke at his house in Westlake when he'd asked, but she'd managed to resist. It seemed premature until Seth knew that Zeke was his father, although she didn't know why they were still holding back.

Perhaps it was because she still didn't know what Zeke had been about to say that night in the chateau, when she'd finally silenced his arguments by making love to him her way.

Or perhaps she was just being over-cautious— Seth was going to have to find out some time— but until she knew exactly how much of a family they were going to be able to be, she didn't want to give her son false expectations.

Or herself.

They'd reached the yacht by now, and even a loudhailer wasn't rousing the skipper.

'I don't want to go alongside in this weather,' Zeke decided. 'Not unless I have to. That yacht is getting thrown around all over the place and the last thing we need is for both boats to be thrown together.'

'I'll go over in an inflatable,' Jonathon, one of the more experienced crewmen, suggested. 'I'll take the tow line across and I can check on the skipper. Then I'll stay below decks with them whilst we start the tow-ride back to Delburn.'

'I'll come with you.' Tia moved alongside Jonathon.

'You stay here for now,' Zeke decided. 'Until we know what state they're in.'

Tia pursed her lips.

'That doesn't make sense. They're likely to be cold and shaken at the very least.'

'Once that yacht is at the end of the line, there's no way to control it or choose which wave it can dodge. It will just have to follow us,' Zeke countered. 'If it goes broadside, that could be the three of you in the water.'

'There was enough of an issue to activate their personal distress beacon. Hypothermia and shock would be my initial concerns. It doesn't make sense to risk the trip across twice.'

She silently willed him to think twice. This was the first shout they'd been on together and if it had been anybody else, she doubted he would have been so reticent. And neither of them wanted their working relationship to be like that.

He scowled briefly, but she could see the exact moment he switched from lover to professional.

'Fine. Get whatever kit you think you could need and we'll see you both over. Once you're there we can shorten the tow if you need anything else, but it's going to be a long ride back.'

'I might be able to temporarily rig the radio somehow through the GPS aerial,' Jonathon suggested.

'Good.' Zeke nodded. 'Okay, get your kit and I'll manoeuvre you as close as I can for launch.'

It was twenty minutes later by the time the two of them reached the yacht and climbed on board, with Jonathon securing the tow as she took the exhausted yachtsman—who had been on deck for their landing—back below deck.

His core temperature was low, but he wasn't yet in hypothermic shock.

'Okay, let's start by you getting out of your wet gear and into some dry clothes whilst I make you a warm, sweet tea.'

'I'd prefer coffee,' he joked weakly, despite his shivering.

'Glad to see you've still got your sense of humour. Coffee it is, then. We can gradually add layers to avoid sending you into thermal shock by heating you up too quickly. And I'm going to set up a saline drip just to be on the safe side. We've got a pretty long tow-ride back.'

'Tow line is set up.' Jonathon dropped below for a moment. 'I'm going to stay here for a little longer to make sure it doesn't part. All we can do now is wait.'

'We can't dodge the waves—we could still capsize,' the yachtsman said quietly.

'It's a possibility,' Tia acknowledged after a moment. 'But we've got one of the best coxswains out there. He'll do everything he can to keep us safe.'

'Yeah, he's going to be missed when he goes on that mission of his next week.'

'What mission?' Tia snapped her head up perhaps a little too quickly, but Jonathon had his back to her and didn't notice.

'You'd have thought he'd had enough of it in the military, wouldn't you? But I guess that's his life, he can't stay away. We always pray he'll come back safely.'

Tia faced him, anger swirling around her like some kind of ballroom dancer with a cape. If it hadn't been the last thing he needed right at this moment, he might have taken a moment longer to admire the sheer force of his wife.

'You can't go back there, Zeke.' However firm, and calm, and rational she was clearly trying to sound, her evident desperation was undermining her. 'Look what happened the last time you were in a place that dangerous.'

He felt guilt and elation all at once. As much as he had no desire to hurt her, it was buoying to see how much she cared. He just needed to allay her fears.

'I have to go out there, Tia. These are *my* men, a close-protection squad who *I* have personally trained, and they've just lost their team commander to something as unforeseeable as a motorbike crash. It has shaken them, and for two of these young men this is their first ever job without the full force of the military behind them.'

'And they think you being out there can protect them?'

It was the disdain in her tone that got to him. A dismissal that his father had perfected. A disregard he had sworn he would never again allow anyone to make him feel.

It was as though his very blood were effervescing. His whole body a mass of coiled nerves. His skin almost too tight to contain it.

He couldn't explain the part of him that wanted to roar at her. To tell her, yes, he could protect them all. Because he knew that was illogical. He couldn't guarantee that.

But he'd feel a damn sight better about sending them out there if he was with them.

'You can't protect everyone, you know,' she hurled at him, as if reading his mind. 'You can't stop something from going wrong, if that's what's going to happen. You should know that better than anyone. Or are you saying that if *your* commanders had been there that night, you would never have lost your leg?'

'Of course not.' The admission felt as though it were being ripped from his mouth. His little Tia made her point a little too well. Worse, she might as well be reading his very soul. 'I'm not going out there to protect them. I'm going out there to appraise them.'

'You keep telling yourself that, Zeke.'

'So, you think I should be happy to send them out there to protect the life of a principal who has virtually no military training, yet cower back because it's *safer*?'

'A principal?'

He grasped it as though it were a lifeline.

'The principal,' he repeated. 'The individual who is paying us to protect them out in an environment which is utterly hostile to them.'

'I know what a damn principal is, Zeke.' Tia raised her voice a notch, clearly unable to stop herself. 'But those men you've trained are all former military. The environment isn't hostile to them.'

'I still know it better,' he barked.

'No.' She shook her head. 'You don't. You and I both know that conflict zones are rapidly changing environments. What worked six months ago, a year ago, two years, won't work any more. Tactics change, old exploits stop working, weaknesses get strengthened. It's why the military always choose a selection of troops fresh out of theatre to train the next deployment to go in. Because their intel and experience is the most up to date and relevant.'

'Which is precisely why I go out there several times a year.'

'But not into direct conflict, Zeke. You go into passive conflict zones. You and I both know there's a difference.'

'Is that what you came down here for, Tia? To chastise me? To remind me that I'm disabled now and try to set limits on me as a result? I thought we got past this. Didn't Look to the Horizon teach you anything about my attitude to my capabilities?'

'My God, Zeke, is that what you really think of me?'

He forced himself to stand still. Not to move or even to blink. Merciless. Pitiless. Which made it all the more incredible when he began to finally talk to her.

'I need this, Tia—you must see that?'

'You need it? You're a multimillionaire. You have Z-Black and Look to the Horizon. Why would you need to put yourself through all that again?'

'Because it makes me feel alive. It reminds me who I am, and what I'm capable of.'

'You make it sound as though, if you don't go out there, you'll be someone different.'

He didn't answer immediately, but then he met her confused gaze.

'Maybe that's what I fear.'

He willed her to understand but she only furrowed her brow all the more.

'I don't understand. If it was so important to you, then why not be one of those hundreds of major limb amputation soldiers who have gone back into service? Some even back into war zones.'

He knew what she was thinking. No doubt as an army doctor she'd seen former soldiers hell-bent on getting back to their buddies, to the only life they'd ever known. He certainly had. And she would know how fired up they could be. How single-mindedly they chased down their goals.

Tia had known him for nearly two decades, she would surely imagine that he would have been worse, or better depending on perspective, than any of them.

'But I was SBS. The kind of things we do—the things I *did*—are demanding enough on the human body when it's at its peak. An operative with one leg…that's a liability.'

'Let me guess, you refused to settle for what you would have seen as second best?'

'I was black ops, of course anything else was always going to feel like second best to me.'

'Really?' She wanted to stop but she couldn't. The words—the hurt—were all there. 'Like a family? Like Seth and me?'

'That's a completely different thing, Tia.'

'Is it?' she challenged. 'Only, from where I'm standing, it feels *exactly* like that. Despite everything we said, and faced up to back at the chateau, for some reason you're still punishing yourself.'

'And you know all this, do you?' He was contemptuous, valiantly trying to ignore the fear that ran beneath the surface, that she might just be right. 'Just because we've been sleeping together for a couple of weeks? Just because I finally let you see my stump?'

She blanched.

It should have felt more of a victory.

'We're going around in circles,' she mumbled

at last. 'Every time I think we've sorted it out, somehow it finds a way to resurrect itself.'

'Maybe that's because I'll never get away from it, Tia. It's who I am. You should know that by now.'

'You need to change,' she announced suddenly.

He didn't know what it was about her tone, but a shiver moved over his entire body.

'Why do I need to change, Tia? For me? Or for you?'

'For my son.'

'*Our* son,' he corrected furiously, a coldness washing through him as she shook her head.

'No.'

It hung between them, casting a shadow that looked bizarrely menacing.

'Yes, Tia. *Our* son. You don't get to shut me out.'

It was the sudden silence that scraped at him, he realised. The awful, bleak, dangerous lack of sound as Tia stared at him wordlessly.

And this time when she spoke, it was the careful, quiet, deadly way she controlled her voice that made the hairs on the back of his arms stand to attention.

'I do. Or, at least, I will do everything within my earthly power to do so.'

'Say again?' His tone was lethal.

'I won't agree to you telling Seth who you are if you go out there.'

'You're threatening me.' He was incredulous.

'I'm warning you,' she corrected. And then, without warning, a sadness crept into her words.

'You aren't listening to me. I told you what I went through with my mum. With you. I can't put my child through that, Zeke. I *won't.*'

Tia stopped, choking on her words and her tears, unable to go on.

She didn't need to. Zeke could hear them, loud and clear, and destructive, echoing around his head.

He had no idea how long they stood there, glaring at each other, her stifled sounds slowly subsiding.

'This is who I am, Tia. This is what I do. It gives me purpose.'

'You have Z-Black,' she croaked. 'Look to the Horizon.'

'I told you, they aren't enough.'

'Seth should be enough. He is four years old.' She dropped her head, the whispered words barely audible. 'He won't cope with losing his father. He won't understand it.'

'We'll explain it to him…' Zeke began, but he already knew that he never would.

'I don't think *I* can understand it…' she choked

out. 'You were *the one*, Zeke. You were always *the one*. There has never been anyone else for me but you, and there never will be.'

Had his chest exploded, right there and then? It felt as if it should have. He had no idea how he managed to stay calm.

'Is that so?'

She swallowed before saying anything more.

'But I can't be with you, Zeke. Not if you go back out on missions again.'

Her words were like a hidden propeller slicing into him again and again. Wounding him, damaging him. He was caught in the momentum and there was no escape.

'Tia, you have to understand why this is so important.'

'I do,' she gasped, as though fighting for every breath. 'I truly do. But you also have to understand that we can't lose you, Zeke.'

Her words struck him, their impact feeling much the same as the time he'd been struck in the Kevlar-protected chest by a shotgun round. How he'd stayed upright was beyond him.

'You won't.'

'You can't guarantee that.'

'And I can't guarantee that I wouldn't walk out of that door and be hit by a speeding motorist.'

'It isn't the same and you know it. One is a

pure freak accident. The other...you're deliberately putting yourself into a hostile environment. I can't have Seth living like that. Always watching the door and wondering.'

'You're telling me not to go.'

'No.' She shook her head sadly. 'I'm desperately hoping that you won't *want* to, any more.'

It was like a black, oily slick, spreading through his body, into his brain, clogging his mouth.

Something in him wanted to oblige. He could feel his throat tightening and loosening as though preparing for the words, but they never came.

All he could do was shake his head. Once. Brusquely. As though that might ease the white light pain slicing through his head.

He heard the sob thicken her throat even as she pushed her words past it, valiantly holding herself together.

'That's what I thought.' The words so sorrowful, so wispy, that he barely heard them before the wind whipped them away.

And when she stumbled away from him, he didn't try to stop her.

CHAPTER FIFTEEN

As the lightweight, fast vessel powered its way through the churning waters, Tia held tightly to the grab-rail and scanned the expanse of water, along with the other three crew members.

There was no sign of their Mayday call-out— a young girl whose dinghy had apparently been swept out of the bay—and Tia's last shout with Delburn Bay's lifeboat crew.

With everything that had happened with Zeke, staying here was no longer an option. The place held almost as many memories for her as West-lake. It was time for a fresh start, in a completely new place. And even if her heart was breaking, she had no time to indulge it; her son needed her to be strong.

He needed her to be good enough to make up the role of two parents. And she wouldn't let him down.

'There, what's that just off your bow?' she yelled, suddenly spotting a movement on the jagged rocks below the towering cliffs that lined up either side of the bay. 'Redheart's Point.'

The crew all peered harder, the glare of the sun off the water hampering their efforts. But eventually Billy, the lifeguard she had met that first day in the office, bobbed his head in agreement.

'There's someone on those rocks and it looks like they're trying to hail us. Have we got any more intel on the scenario?'

'Nothing. I'm taking her in,' the helmsman concurred, as he turned the boat and headed towards the cliffs.

Tia pursed her lips. This was a dangerous stretch of coast. The water was never very deep and the wrecks of multiple fishing boats posed an additional danger to the hull of their lifeboat. But there was no way down to, or up from, the beach at Redheart's Point. And twice a day it got swallowed up by the tide. Whoever was waving to them would have no way off their rapidly shrinking beach if her lifeboat crew didn't get in to them.

Dan, their helmsman, made several attempts, but the swell kept lifting and buffeting them, threatening to smash them against the small jagged rocks that occasionally tipped their sharp heads above the swirling water, like razor fish coming to the surface of the sand.

'We could veer out?' Billy suggested.

Dan shook his head.

'There's too much submerged just below the boat. It's too great a risk.'

'I don't mind getting in and heading onto the beach,' Tia suggested.

'You stay here,' Vinny, the third crew member, jumped in immediately. 'It's bad enough that you're leaving. We can't have anything happening to you, as well.'

'Funny.' Tia punched him lightly on the arm, but it was heartening to hear she would be missed. Her ego could do with a bit of massaging at the moment.

'Wait, let these three waves go and then I'll get you as close as possible.' Dan delayed his crewman. 'We'll come in as soon as you radio us.'

'Stay safe,' Tia instructed as Vinny began to scramble over the side.

They watched as he braced himself and dropped into the water.

'"Smoke me a kipper,"' he quoted, taking the bag Billy was passing him and getting clear of the boat before a wave smashed him against it.

Tia watched, her heart racing, as he made slow progress through the swell, almost being knocked off his feet twice in the first minute alone.

As hairy as it was, though, Tia welcomed the challenge. It was better than being consumed with thoughts of Zeke, and how she and Seth hadn't been enough to keep him home. Keep him safe.

Suddenly, Dan edged up in his seat.

'I think there are two casualties.'

'Say again?' Moving across the boat, Tia put her head by his shoulder to follow the direction of his hand.

'There. Beyond the girl who was signalling. Is that another figure on the rocks? Lying down?'

'I see it.' Tia nodded. 'Definitely another person. Dan, I have to go with Vinny, and I'm going to take the spinal board.'

'Then I'm going with you.' Billy jerked upright so fast the boat rocked. 'There's no way you can get through that surf with a kit bag and a seven-foot board on your own.'

'Fine.' Tia nodded. 'Okay, Dan? Good, let's go.'

It took another twelve chilling minutes before she was grasping Vinny's hand and he was hauling her and the spinal board onto the rocky beach. Billy was seconds behind.

'Tread carefully,' Vinny warned. 'These rocks are particularly slippery. Okay, so casualties are

Rebecca, eighteen, and her sixteen-year-old sister, Amy. They were both in the dinghy when it got caught by the wind and swept out of the bay. They ended up just off the shore here where the tide drove them to these rocks.'

Tia followed Vinny across the rocks as quickly and carefully as she could, with both Vinny and Billy carrying the board.

'They got caught up in a swell just as they were coming in and the dinghy capsized. Amy was thrown cleanly into the water, but Rebecca was thrown onto something. She made it ashore but she's complaining of severe pain in her neck. They've tried to lie her down as flat as they can, but it's just not possible on the rocks.'

'Okay, thanks.' Tia hurried over to the sisters. 'Hi, Amy, is it? My colleague Billy is going to check you out. I'm Tia, I'm a doctor. I'm going to look after your sister. Rebecca, can you tell me where it hurts?'

Carefully, Tia carried out a check of Rebecca, ascertaining pain in the girl's left buttock and leg and an inability to move her left leg.

'Okay, Rebecca, flower, you're doing really well. I'm going to give you something to help with the pain and then we're going to try to get you onto a spinal board. I'm going to have to cut away your wet clothes as well.'

She glanced over to where Billy was holding up a blanket to afford the sister a degree of privacy whilst she also got out of her wet things and into the insulating bag that he had pulled out of his kit.

His signal reassured Tia that, other than treatment to prevent hypothermia, he was confident there were no other medical concerns with the younger girl.

She turned to Vinny. 'I'm going to administer some pain relief and let Dan know to scramble the coastguard's search and rescue heli. I don't want to risk trying to transfer her via board and boat, with her paralysis and neurological deficit. Can you look after Rebecca here, and then we'll get Billy to help us put her on a spinal board?'

'Yeah. Guess your last day is going out with a bang, then.' He lifted his eyebrows. 'Not exactly what you had in mind when you came in this morning?'

'Not at all.' Tia exhaled. 'But as long as we get them away safely, that's all that matters.'

When the door opened, she didn't even bother to turn around. It would only be another person asking why she was leaving, telling her that she should stay.

She didn't want to hear either. There was only one person she'd ever wanted to hear from. And he hadn't wanted to say the words.

'I hear you're leaving.'

Tia froze. The familiar, uncompromisingly male voice rooting her to the spot. It took her a few long moments to answer.

'Yes.'

Another silence stretched between them.

'You shouldn't. You're good here. You fit in.'

Each sentence was like a lash, whipping her with its polite evenness. Wholly unemotional.

'I can be a medical advisor somewhere else. Coming back here was…a bad idea.'

'Coming back here was brave,' he corrected.

'No, it was foolish.'

And desperate, not that she was about to add that last bit. Instead, she wondered if the silence that once again descended were a black cloak, would she be able to lose herself for good?

Instead, Tia forced herself to turn around. She wasn't prepared for the way her heart slammed against her chest wall.

His voice might be inscrutable, collected, but his appearance was anything but.

Dark shadows ringed eyes that didn't look

as though they'd slept in days whilst an even darker shadow veiled his jaw; making it seem even more square, even more male, than ever. Irrationally, she ached to reach out and touch it, to let it graze her soft skin as though the abrasion could make her *feel* something, anything, after a month of feeling numb.

She had no idea how she pulled herself together.

'If it wasn't foolish, then tell me what it was, Zeke.' She was proud of the way her voice didn't crack and completely betray her. 'What are you doing back here? I thought you were going for three months, not one. Or is this a couple of days' break to check on your business?'

Without warning, he raked his hand through his hair. It was a gesture so unsure, so unfamiliar, so wholly un-Zeke-like that it made her breath catch in her throat.

'I love you.'

'I know,' she whispered. 'Just not enough.'

'Enough that I'm not going back.'

It was so simple, so sure, so unexpected, that she felt as though she must be swaying, right there where she stood. And how she stayed upright defied belief. She had to caution her fickle heart.

'This time. But what about next time, or the one after that?'

'Enough that I will never leave you—or Seth—again. I will never go back into a conflict zone.'

The words tossed into the air, like the spray from the sea as it crashed wave after wave down on the shoreline outside the window, beyond where Zeke stood. And Tia found she was staring at it as though she were reading the words in the surf rather than hearing them coming from his mouth itself.

It was surreal. And perfect. And almost too much to hope for.

'I want to believe you,' she muttered softly, 'so much.'

'You should.'

Tia hesitated. She felt raw, scraped through. Emotionally wrung out like an exhausted swimmer caught in a riptide and barely able to keep their head above water whilst they prayed for help to arrive.

'Why?' she whispered at last.

'Because you were right, I was pushing myself, trying to prove myself to a ghost of a man to whom I should never have even given a second thought. It gave me a battle to distract myself. Without it, I might have just given up.'

She couldn't imagine Zeke, so ruthless, so strong, ever giving up on anything.

Except her.

And now he was telling her that he hadn't even done that.

'What changed?'

'You. Telling me that I didn't need all of *that* to feel alive. Showing me that I had you. And Seth. A family.'

'I told you that a month ago. You left anyway.'

'Because I was an idiot.'

'You were,' she agreed, then offered an unexpected, if weak, smile. 'But you aren't the only one. You were right, you know?'

'I was right? I like the sound of that.'

'Don't get used to it,' she tried to joke feebly. 'But you accused me once of being just as closed off as you. There I was, blaming you for shutting me out and not trusting me. But I was doing exactly the same to you.'

'Your mother.'

'Yes.' She nodded, trying to swallow down the painful lump currently wedged in her throat. 'Her death devastated me, we were so close. I needed to talk about her and honour her, but my father found it too painful, and so I had to stay silent. I felt as though we were pretending she didn't exist and I know I resented him for it.'

'So dating me *was* a way to rebel.' He didn't sound sad, or angry, but that didn't make her feel any better.

'I suppose it was a bit of that. It was my way of getting my own back on him. But it was also a bit of the other thing you once said. The "running away from our pasts" bit.'

'And are you still doing that?'

Taut lines radiated from his face. Her answer mattered to him.

It mattered to her, as well.

'No, I'm not. At least, I'm trying not to. When I lost you, I knew I needed to make a change. I finally asked my father about my mother and he started to tell me. Only a little at first—it isn't easy for him and after all this time it isn't easy for me either—but enough. Then the next time I visited, he had a few photos and some little anecdotes to go with it.'

'I'm so glad, Tia.'

'Yes.' His obvious care made her feel more cherished than he'd ever made her feel before. 'It's going to take time, but we're getting there. Soon I can start sharing little memories with Seth. I think he should know a little about my mother and how much of a hero she was.'

'I think he would like that.'

'And…and I'd like to start sharing what I've

learned with you, too. Maybe even work on getting a plaque dedicated to her and her crew.'

'They want one, you know. At Westlake. There are a couple of old-timers there who even still remember working with her. But your father always shot the idea down.'

It was almost too much. She swallowed once. Twice. But the heavy ball of emotion was still there, lodged in her throat.

'I didn't know,' she admitted. 'But it sounds lovely.'

'It is. But don't rush at it, Tia. Go at your own pace. The crew will understand. Everyone will.'

'Thank you, I…just thank you,' she managed. 'So you've really come home?'

'For good. The only travelling I intend to do now is to the chateau. I've done my bit. I've laid down my life for people for years. Now the only people I'm prepared to give my life for are my wife and son.'

'Do you really mean that?'

'I spent five years buried beneath my despair, using my company and my charity to distract me from what I didn't want to face. But this past month without you, or Seth, was worse than all of that put together. You make me a better version of myself, Tia. The kind of man I never knew I wanted to become.'

'And it took you a month to realise that?'

'Not quite. But I had to get a new guy out and bring him up to speed. He's the new team leader now. The wait damn near killed me.'

'If you'd listened to me in the first place, you wouldn't have had to,' she teased, scarcely able to believe what he was saying. 'You *are* an idiot.'

'But I seem to remember you telling me a few weeks ago that I could be *your* idiot.'

'You remember that, huh?' She laughed, a shaky but genuine sound.

Her eyes prickled and something inside her began to unfurl and warm her, the heat penetrating right through to her icy bones.

'I will never forget it again,' he promised her solemnly, finally closing the gap between them and taking her face in his hands. 'Will you?'

'Never,' she breathed, placing her hands flat on Zeke's solid chest to reassure herself that she wasn't dreaming.

'Kiss me,' he commanded. 'So I know this is real.'

As though he had read her mind.

And Tia was only too happy to oblige. She pushed herself up onto her toes, her hands gliding up the reassuringly hard ridges and planes and winding around Zeke's neck. She shivered as their lips met, his mouth so demanding, crushing hers so that pleasure and pain intertwined. Finally she melted as he pulled her body to his, fitting it to him as though they had been hand-crafted to be together.

For ever.

'I only have one amendment to make to your promise to lay down your life for no one else but Seth and me,' she murmured softly when they finally resurfaced a lifetime later.

'Really?' he managed abstractly. His teeth nipped at her neck, his hands moving over her as though he was trying to assure himself he hadn't forgotten a single detail whilst he'd been away. 'And what's that?'

'That you'll also protect any sister or brother Seth might have.'

Zeke stopped, his head lifting slowly and his eyes coming to meet hers. There was no doubting the love shining from them. So bright, so strong, it was almost blinding.

'You want another baby with me?' He sounded almost awed.

'I do. Don't you?'

'More than anything,' he assured her gruffly. 'When do you want to start? This year? Next?'

'How about now? Or at least…when we get home?'

'Home?'

'To Westlake. There's a house on a plot over-looking the sea, where I always wanted to live.'

'Convenient.'

'I thought so.'

And then he groaned slightly with the effort of pulling away from her, enveloped her hand in his, and finally took her home.

* * * * *

LET'S TALK

Romance

For exclusive extracts, competitions and special offers, find us online:

f facebook.com/millsandboon

⊙ @millsandboonuk

🐦 @millsandboon

Or get in touch on 0844 844 1351*

For all the latest titles coming soon, visit millsandboon.co.uk/nextmonth